ELF PRINCE

ELF PRINCE

AN ELVEN ALLIANCE NOVEL

TARA GRAYCE

Elf Prince

Copyright © 2022 by Tara Grayce

Taragrayce.com

Published by Sword & Cross Publishing

Grand Rapids, MI

Sword & Cross Publishing and the Sword & Cross Publishing logo are trademarks. Absence of ™ in connection with Sword & Cross Publishing does not indicate an absence of trademark protection of those marks.

Cover Illustration by Sara Morello

www.deviantart.com/samo-art

Typography by Deranged Doctor Designs

Derangeddoctordesign.com

Map by Savannah Jezowski of Dragonpen Designs

Dragonpenpress.com

To God, my King and Father. Soli Deo Gloria

LCCN: 2022906421

ISBN: 978-1-943442-25-6

THE WORLD OF ELVEN ALLIANCE

AUTHOR'S NOTE

I originally wrote *Elf Prince* as a freebie novella to give away to newsletter subscribers. It retold the beginning of *Fierce Heart* from Farrendel's point of view and helped me hone his voice before I wrote his chapters of *War Bound*.

Due to popular demand, I kept slowly adding chapters to this novella until I had retold the entirety of *Fierce Heart* from Farrendel's POV. As I didn't want this to simply be a re-hash, I tried to stick with adding new scenes of things that were skipped over in *Fierce Heart*. But many key scenes were retold with the dialogue remaining word-for-word. I hope you all still enjoy this book, even if you already know what happens. Farrendel's internal monologue is always so much fun, and it was great to see how both he and Essie approached their relationship from their individual perspectives.

This book was written with the understanding that you have already read *Fierce Heart*. It will likely make more sense that way.

If you want to read *Fierce Heart* and *Elf Prince* side by side to get the full effect of the dual POVs, you can find a printable side-by-side chapter list on my website on my Extras page: https://taragrayce.com/extras/

ONE

F arrendel Laesornysh, prince of the elves of
Tarenhiel, sank into the burning roar of his
magic. Blue bolts of power surrounded him,
flaring out to lash at the trolls who had unwisely invaded
across the border from their kingdom of Kostaria.

A line of trolls raised muskets and fired, all of them
aiming for Farrendel.

Farrendel flicked his fingers and sent a blast of his
magic surging forward. The magic incinerated the musket
balls into dust and smoke before bursting against the
trolls who had fired, hurling them to the ground and
against the trunks of trees several yards from where they
had knelt.

A few rocks hurtled through the air on a wave of icy
troll magic and peppered against Farrendel's shield,
lacking the strength to make his magic so much as falter.

Farrendel glanced over his shoulder to the far side of
the forest meadow where his brother Weylind led the
border patrol in holding back the left flank of the troll

regiment while Farrendel alone fought the right and most of the center.

Weylind flipped over a wall of rock that a pack of trolls had magically shoved from the ground. With his long sword flashing in one hand, Weylind unleashed a wave of his own magic. Roots burst from the ground, crumbling the rock wall into pebbles. The trees at the edge of the meadow lashed forward with their branches, knocking into the trolls trying to circle around Weylind's warriors.

Good. Weylind had the battle well in hand on that side of the meadow. Not that Farrendel should have doubted him. Before Farrendel had come into his magic as he matured, Weylind had been the foremost warrior among the elves, back when Weylind had been the crown prince while his and Farrendel's father still lived.

His father. Farrendel gritted his teeth, the ache from his father's death burning in his chest. He refused to feel the pain of watching his father die. Not even while fighting the trolls, his father's killers.

His magic tried to crackle farther, brighter, but he held it in check, not letting the depth of his emotions cause him to lose control over the blasts of power. If he did not keep his magic under tight control, he could end up killing Weylind and all the elven warriors fighting with them, not to mention level this entire section of forest, including the nearby village that Farrendel, Weylind, and the warriors were protecting.

Still, he was done with this battle. He had held back, giving these trolls a chance to surrender or retreat to Kostaria if they wished.

He released a little more of his magic, the bolts of power sizzling hotter, slicing sharper. He lashed the bolts forward, taking out the first line of trolls who had regathered and tried to charge him again.

They fell, the magic slicing through their armor, down through bone and muscle and blood until it stabbed their hearts.

Farrendel refused to let his stomach churn. Refused to feel the way each death shuddered into his own soul. This was why he had earned the elven name Laesornysh, meaning *Death on the Wind.* His magic made killing quick. Efficient.

He was a weapon. Nothing more.

He allowed the next pack of trolls to charge him, closing the distance. When they were mere feet away, he drew his two swords from his back and ran at them with a flying leap. He plunged a sword into the first troll's chest, then used the falling body to spring into the air, coming down on the shoulders of the next troll.

With magic coating his blades, he spun and flipped in the air, parrying the swords thrust at him, blocking the troll magic hurled at him, and thrusting his swords into his attackers.

By the time his feet touched the ground again, that ground was littered with bodies, forming lumps among the trees and on the grass of the meadow. Not one troll remained of the raiding party.

A massacre. And he had been the one to cause it.

Farrendel lowered his arms, letting the crackle of his killing magic dissipate. With his emotions locked in an icy place in his chest, he cleaned his swords using the jerkin of the nearest body before sheathing them.

Around the meadow and the edges of the forest, the other elf warriors fanned out, checking that all the trolls were dead. They were. Farrendel knew that already.

Footsteps brushed the grass behind him. Weylind, his brother and the king of Tarenhiel, halted beside him, his sword also once again sheathed. Weylind's gaze flicked over the destruction. "It is worrisome that they attacked in such great numbers the day before our diplomatic meeting with Escarland's king. While I do not believe that meeting is a great secret, I did not think the trolls had the resources to learn of it."

As the trolls' kingdom of Kostaria occupied the far north while Escarland lay to the south, the two kingdoms did not share a border. News of happenings in Escarland would have to go through Tarenhiel to reach Kostaria, unless Kostaria had dealings with the kingdoms to the far west.

Something for consideration, though they had little time to dwell on it now.

Farrendel clasped his hands behind his back, trying to ignore the urge to rub his stained fingers against his tunic until all the blood was cleaned away. "Perhaps they wished to delay us from reaching our meeting with Escarland. The trolls would only benefit from a renewal of our war with the humans."

War on two borders. Tarenhiel had fought such a war only fifteen years before, beset both by the trolls from Kostaria in the north and the humans from Escarland in the south, though Kostaria and Escarland had never allied together against Tarenhiel. Only the death of the kings of all three kingdoms had halted that series of wars, bringing about the uneasy peace, punctuated by frequent raids, that had occurred in the years since.

But as tensions were escalating with the trolls, it was imperative that peace be made with Escarland. Tarenhiel could not risk splitting its forces again, and Farrendel could not lose his brother to a war as he had already lost his father.

Weylind gave a short nod. "Yes. After the months it took to arrange this meeting, King Averett of the humans would be affronted if we arrived late or missed it altogether. The trolls must know this, somehow."

Either that, or they simply had really inconvenient timing. As it was, Farrendel and Weylind would have to board the train as soon as possible and travel through the night to cross the length of Tarenhiel and reach the meeting place at the southern border with Escarland in time.

Another war to avert. Another war Farrendel would have to fight if they did not.

A tremble shook his hand, but he clenched his fists tighter. He could not allow himself to break. Not yet.

Weylind spun, giving orders to the warrior in charge, before he and Farrendel headed to the stand of trees where they had left their horses. Farrendel did not envy the warriors left behind, who would have the task of burying the dead, then returning to their patrol along the border.

It was a short ride on horseback to the nearest train station where they had left the royal train. Farrendel climbed into his private car, locking the door behind him.

Only now could he break. His hands shook as he dashed to the shower in the water closet. Turning on the water as hot as the train's water system could produce, he stood under the shower's spray, blood-spattered clothes and all, and let it wash off the blood.

So much blood. In his clothes. On his skin. Clumped in the long strands of his silver-blond hair. He scrubbed and scrubbed. First his clothes, then his skin, until his

5

skin shone red and raw. And still he could not feel clean.

Blood. Death. He could still taste it. Smell it.

His stomach churned, and he had to brace himself against the wall, heaving deep breaths as he struggled not to vomit.

He hated war. Hated death.

He could not do this much longer. He was so tired. Everything in him was broken.

What choice did he have? He could not allow Taren-hiel to fall. His brother needed him to fight, and he could not refuse, knowing Weylind had a greater chance of dying on the battlefield if he did. With his destructive magic and his illegitimate birth, it was not as if Farrendel was good for anything besides fighting and killing.

This was his life. Fight. Kill. And, eventually, die.

*P*AIN STABBED BENEATH HIS SKIN. *He lay flat on his back, each breath constricted against the stone binding him to the floor. Darkness crept through him, capturing him in a painful haze between unconsciousness and wakefulness.*

A hand touched his shoulder. He screamed at the agony and tried to thrash away. They were back. More torture. More pain.

"Farrendel, sason."

His father's voice. He struggled toward it. Toward the first gentle hand he had felt in far too many days. How long had it been? He did not know.

He blinked. A form knelt over him. His father's long black hair blurred with the darkness surrounding them. His drawn face sharpened above Farrendel, and it took all of Farrendel's strength to force out a single word. "Dacha."

"I need you to be brave for a while longer, sason." His father's hand tightened on Farrendel's shoulder.

An elf warrior joined Dacha, carrying a chisel and hammer. Each blow, each swing at the rock binding him, tore through his skin, his bones.

But he could not scream. It would bring the trolls running.

Tears streamed down his face. His father's eyes shimmered wet in the torchlight even as he held Farrendel down.

When his father lifted him from the floor, Farrendel had to press his face into his father's shoulder to stifle a scream. His head pounded. Stone burned beneath his skin.

Light seared his eyes as his father stepped from the cave. A battle raged around them. One of the elven warriors surrounding them staggered and fell, an arrow in his back.

Farrendel tried to dredge up his magic, whimpering with pain at the attempt. Too much stone and troll magic beneath his skin.

Across the battlefield, Weylind led a charge, a wedge of warriors sweeping in his wake.

His father took a step. Toward Weylind and safety.

Then there was a horrible thunking sound. A choking gasp. His father dropped to his knees, his grip slackening on Farrendel.

"Dacha!" Farrendel gripped his father in shaking arms. An arrow stuck from his father's back. The light in his father's eyes was fading, his breaths gasping and blood-filled. He shouted for help. Tried to dredge up enough magic to stop the gathering trolls. Pain flared through his body, until the darkness threatened to drag him under again even as his father gasped out his final words.

"Never forget you are my son."

Farrendel bolted upright, heart pounding, gasping for breath. The taste of blood still coated his tongue, even though he had washed several times since the battle. Or perhaps it was the blood and torture of that night fifteen years ago haunting his nightmares still.

Outside the train's rows of windows set into the silver, curving frame of the sleek train car, the forest flashed by, still shadowed in the early morning gray.

He would not sleep more tonight. At least this nightmare was a mild one. If Weylind should overhear his screams during one of his more terrible nightmares, Weylind would realize the extent to which Farrendel still struggled. His brother would pull him from the war, make him stay home and away from fighting and killing.

As much as Farrendel hated all of it, he would not risk Weylind going into battle alone.

After sliding out of bed, Farrendel opened the window set in the roof and boosted himself up and onto the roof. He wore only the trousers he slept in, his feet and chest bare. The cool, early summer breeze blasted his face, dried the sweat from his skin, and whipped his hair behind him, tearing away the last shreds of his nightmare.

He balanced lightly in a crouch, facing forward. Ahead, the branches of the forest hung low over the train, growing in curving arches to allow the train to pass with minimal disturbance to the forest.

The first tree branch whipped at him knee high. He jumped over it and immediately dropped as the next one aimed right at his head. He twisted between the next two, then vaulted off one of the lower branches to clear a higher one before landing lightly on the train's roof once again.

He fell into a rhythm. Not thinking. Not feeling. Pushing his reflexes and strength as hard as he could.

As dawn broke across the horizon to the east, the trees

thinned until the broad expanse of the Hydalla River, the border between Tarenhiel and Escarland, spread in a rippling line as far as he could see in both directions. In the distance, he spotted the lump of Linder Island jutting from the center of the river. It was nothing but a large rock breaking the flow of the river, but in a few hours, it would become the host of the first diplomatic meeting between Tarenhiel and Escarland in fifteen years.

Farrendel stood, balancing lightly on the top of the train, and peered across the morning-shadowed river toward the hazy gray bank on the far side. Escarland. If this diplomatic meeting failed, there was a good chance he would be called on to hold back the Escarlish armies from crossing that river. The river would run red with blood, choked with bodies.

That was not a future he ever wanted to see. Whatever it took today, whatever Escarland demanded, they needed peace at this border. One war was already breaking him. He could not fight two.

As much as he would rather linger here, with the breeze cooling his sweat-dampened skin, Weylind would come looking for him shortly to discuss final details before they left. Not that Farrendel had many duties for this meeting. He was simply there to watch for treachery on the part of the humans and deal with it swiftly and lethally if it occurred.

The burden of the negotiation would rest on Weylind and Sindrel, an elf scholar who had spent a century studying human customs. While both Weylind and Farrendel could read Escarlish, Sindrel had studied human legal contracts and would be better able to understand any confusing language the humans might use to slip trickery into the treaty itself.

Never trust a human bargain. That was the common saying, after all. Humans lied. They treated words flippantly. Everyone knew humans were a treacherous, deceitful race. The trolls to the north were fierce enemies, but at least they had their code that they honored.

Humans did not even have that. Humans claimed honor, only to throw it away the first chance they had.

Farrendel shook his head and dropped through the hatch into his private train car. He needed to wash now so that his hair would have time to dry before the meeting. He might as well start the day clean. There was a good chance he would end it blood-spattered and unclean all the way to his soul.

After eating cold meat and cheese stocked in the magically chilled cupboard in his train car, he stepped into the water closet's shower and scrubbed until the sweat and memories of the nightmare were gone from his skin. As he washed, he felt the train slowing and stopping at the station, the end of the line for this particular set of tracks.

Once dressed in the silver tunic and trousers he would wear for the meeting, he left his train car and entered the seating car, a train car with benches on either side and long banks of windows giving a view of the river.

There, Sindrel and Weylind were already gathered, talking quietly. Weylind glanced up and met Farrendel's gaze. "The humans sent word their king is bringing his sister to the diplomatic meeting this morning. We have yet to determine what trick they may be playing with this."

It had to be a trick. The humans never did anything without an angle for themselves. "Perhaps they wish to lure us into a sense of safety before they attempt an attack."

Sindrel shook his head, his brown hair sliding across his shoulders. "While humans are known to be treacherous, I do not believe they would bring a princess along if they were planning a physical attack. They have a strange honor code when it comes to their women. They believe women should not physically fight nor witness war. That especially holds true for their royalty."

Farrendel shook his head. He had known many elven female warriors. He had fought alongside them. Been saved by them. While female warriors were not as common as male warriors, it was not something their society opposed, as it seemed human culture did.

"If this is a trick to lure us into a false sense of safety, the trick will most likely lie in the treaty itself. Perhaps they believe this princess of theirs will be a distraction so that we do not notice some trick of the wording they intend to write into the treaty." Sindrel tapped his fingers against his leg, as if mentally counting the different Escarlish words he needed to watch for that day. "Though it does seem strange, given the last war, that they would bring their princess along. They must assume there is a likelihood of this meeting ending in battle."

"Perhaps they believe her presence will prevent us from attacking them." Weylind crossed his arms. "They plan to stand behind their princess as a shield."

"That is a possibility." Sindrel's face darkened. "Humans usually do not bring their women to battle, but if this human king hates elves enough, he may be willing to risk his sister and attack us anyway, knowing we would be averse to fighting with her present."

Farrendel's stomach churned. Fighting the female troll warriors was one thing. They were trained, and they took up weapons in full knowledge of what it could cost. But if this human princess was an innocent who ended up caught in the middle of fighting, that would be something different. He was not sure he could bear it if he lost control of his magic and harmed an innocent.

More blood on his hands. Soaking into his skin. He clenched his fists, resisting the urge to scrub his arms yet again. It was never enough. No matter how hard he scraped, he could never wash away the nagging uncleanness of the blood he carried on his hands.

Weylind sighed. "Unless we wish to surrender any hope of a peaceful resolution to this tension, we must attend this diplomatic meeting and face whatever treachery the humans have planned when it comes."

Farrendel dipped his head in a nod. Right now, they could only hope that whatever the humans wanted, the price would not be too high. They were prepared to give the humans whatever they wished, or very nearly so.

It was a surrender, of sorts. A temporary appeasement. Everyone knew the humans would just come back again and again, demanding even more each time.

But what Tarenhiel needed right now was time. Time enough to defeat the trolls and strengthen that border so that when the time came to stop appeasing the humans and start fighting them, Tarenhiel would be in a position to do so victoriously.

TWO

Farrendel disembarked from the boat that had carried them from the larger ship, his swords strapped to his back. Beside him, Iyrinder, the other elf guard chosen for this task, tightened his grip on his strung bow, his jaw set. Weylind and Sindrel stood in front of them, though with space left between them for Iyrinder and Farrendel to jump forward to defend them if necessary.

Across the tiny rock island, the humans from Escarland stepped from their rowboat. Among the men was a young woman dressed in a gown with a massive blue skirt that set off the fiery red of her hair. As the only female human among the group, she must be their princess.

As they neared, she glanced up at Weylind and smiled. A genuine smile that sparkled in her eyes and rounded her cheeks. As if she was pleased to be meeting elves on this island.

Who was this human princess that she would smile

so? How did she manage to smile with such joy when facing those who were her enemies?

Her gaze swiveled past Weylind to land first on Iyrinder, then on Farrendel.

He stared back, frozen under her gaze. Should he attempt a smile back? Was this friendliness on her part a trick by the humans?

She blinked, shuddered, and hurriedly looked away.

He had scared her. He had not meant to. But he had been told his gaze carried the hard weight of the death he had seen and caused.

Farrendel stayed to the side as the official greetings were performed and the meeting tent and furniture were set up and arranged. The human king, a man with neatly trimmed auburn hair and hazel eyes, had brought with him seven guards, all of whom eyed Farrendel as if sensing he was the greatest threat there.

Farrendel could not spot any attempt at treachery thus far. Despite their edginess, none of the guards lifted their guns from their shoulders to attempt to take a shot at Weylind. Not that it would do them any good. Farrendel would incinerate the bullet before it came anywhere near his brother.

When Weylind took his seat across the table from King Averett, Farrendel positioned himself at Weylind's back with Iyrinder standing behind Sindrel. Surprisingly, King Averett opted for only two bodyguards of his own and ordered the rest to stand outside the tent. Was it a show of good faith on his part? Or one of the human tricks of which Farrendel needed to be wary?

As a silence fell in the tent, Farrendel braced himself, ready to call up his magic in a moment's notice.

In front of him, Weylind's shoulders tensed a fraction, even as he remained silent.

The silence seemed to make the humans uncomfortable. The red-haired princess's smile wavered. Beside the king, the human diplomat, a small man with brown hair, opened and closed his mouth.

In the center of the table, King Averett made a noise in the back of his throat, shifted, then faced Weylind. "We both know why we are here. The incidents lately have been deplorable, on both sides, and I have made it clear to my people, as I am sure you have to yours, that further action will not be tolerated."

He had made it clear to his people? Farrendel's jaw tightened. Escarland had been the one provoking these incidents. Surely this king was behind it, encouraging the raids even as he publicly denied them. Yet another example of humans saying one thing while doing another.

King Averett waved in the direction of the Escarlish shore. "I have the bodies of your two young elves to return to you with due honor, as I believe you have the bodies of three of my young men."

The three Escarlish men had been killed when a party of ten of them had raided one of the elven villages near the river. An elf had been killed, and some of the young elf males of the village had retaliated with a raid of their own, ending with two elves killed across the border in Escarland. If raids like this continued, it would drag them to war whether or not they wanted it.

"The exchange will occur once our negotiations are complete," Weylind said evenly.

It would do no good to negotiate for the return of the

bodies now when this meeting could very well end in more bloodshed and bodies.

King Averett shifted again, a display of emotion no elf king would allow himself in front of enemies. Though, how much of this open emotion was real and how much was merely a disguise for the treachery he was planning?

When King Averett drew in a deep breath in preparation to speak, Farrendel braced himself. Whatever this human king said next would be the start of whatever ploy they had planned.

"Things have been unsettled between our two kingdoms ever since the end of the war. After a war between two human nations, normally we would seal the new treaty with a marriage alliance to guarantee peace." King Averett gazed at Weylind, his tone and eyes unwavering.

What sort of trick was this? A marriage alliance?

Farrendel had heard stories of human kingdoms engaging in this practice. But he had thought those merely stories. Surely the humans were not so cold-hearted as to bargain their sisters and daughters away in heartless matches such as the ones told in the stories.

He allowed his gaze to flick to the princess. Was she the one her brother was offering for the alliance? Her smile remained in place. If anything, it had tipped higher, as if she found something in this conversation amusing. Certainly she would not be so relaxed and happy if she were the object of this proposed, forced marriage.

King Averett's expression was wiped free of all emotion. "But that is a solution your kingdom hasn't appeared open to exploring in the past."

There was a challenge to his words. As if daring them to take him up on his offer. What game were the humans playing? Did they want Weylind to take the bait or not?

Perhaps it was the challenge that spurred Farrendel into speaking. Maybe it was his own desperation to prevent more blood on his hands. Either way, he surprised even himself when he blurted out, in Escarlish, no less, "Would a marriage alliance stop the raids?"

All eyes swiveled toward him. It took everything in him not to flinch away from all the attention. The human princess's eyes—a light blue-green as he was now close enough to see—widened, and they had a speculative gleam as she studied him.

"Brother, do you believe we should consider this...offer?"

Farrendel dropped his gaze to Weylind, almost relieved to look away from the human princess.

Weylind's jaw tightened. "This must be a trap of some kind. We cannot trust them."

Never trust a human bargain. Farrendel sneaked a glance at the humans, hoping that none of them understood elvish. "We planned to agree to whatever was necessary to appease them. We should hear them out before we refuse. Besides, this is most likely a bluff they hope we will refuse. It would give them cause to label us as uncooperative diplomatically."

Something King Averett could spin as a reason for war. Or, at the very least, a reason to ask for more when he demanded appeasement.

There was nothing they could do but call the human king's bluff and see if that uncovered his real intentions.

Sindrel glanced between Weylind and Farrendel, as if reluctant to interrupt. But when Weylind glanced at him, Sindrel tipped his head in a nod. He must agree with Farrendel that playing along with this bluff would be better than challenging it.

Weylind turned back to King Averett. "Would a marriage alliance as you propose guarantee peace between our kingdoms?"

King Averett flinched, his skin paling, before sharing a look with his sister. The humans were so expressive that it was difficult to tell if this was a genuine reaction or feigned. In an elf, such a display of emotion would have been the work of a bad actor over exaggerating his role for comedic effect.

Was this an over exaggeration to disguise the fact that King Averett had been hoping they would take his bait and step into whatever trap he had laid with proposing a marriage alliance? Or was this real emotion because his plans had been foiled?

Weylind's voice turned hard. "Unless you were not genuine in your offer. We would take it very unkindly if your gestures of peace turn out to be empty."

Ah, good. His brother was taking the opportunity to push the humans, hopefully to force their true purpose to the surface.

King Averett appeared genuinely uncomfortable now, squirming in his seat like he had been caught in his own trap. The human diplomat had paled and kept glancing at his king as if seeking guidance.

The marriage alliance had to have been a bluff of some kind. The humans were too uncomfortable now that Weylind had stepped out of whatever trap they had been laying.

The human princess, however, was the only one not squirming like bait on a hook. Instead, something in her expression glittered as she raised her chin. "Yes, we are genuine in our offer."

She said it with confidence, as if she was the driving

force behind this marriage alliance idea. Unlike all those stories about human princesses forced unwillingly into marriage, was she perhaps volunteering willingly for this?

Farrendel caught his breath, stomach churning. What if this marriage alliance was truly what the humans wanted? This could be the cost they demanded for peace, and their show of reluctance was just that. A show. A means to convince Weylind to agree.

If this princess was the Escarlish side of the marriage, that could only mean one thing: Farrendel was the other half. Weylind, after all, only had one brother.

Unless the humans would be content with a high-ranking lord. Did they even know Weylind had a brother? It was not like Farrendel's existence was something Taren-hiel had celebrated, given his illegitimacy.

Would the humans even want to marry their princess to him if they knew? He was a prince only because his father had been honorable enough to claim him and make him a real part of the family. By all rights, he should have been raised on the streets in some border town, a pauper scraping by for his existence, never knowing his father had been the king of the elves.

The human diplomat made that strange sound in the back of his throat. "Generally, a marriage alliance would include our princess marrying one of your princes while one of your princesses would marry a prince from Escarland."

Farrendel noted the wording. Yes, the Escarlish wanted an elf prince for their human princess, but they did not appear to be certain there was an elf prince available.

Weylind's tone remained cool, the set of his shoulders stiff. "No. I will not marry my sister to a human."

Farrendel could not allow himself to be hurt by Weylind's words. Weylind hadn't objected to a marriage alliance for Farrendel. Just for their sisters, Melantha and Jalissa.

He understood. Agreed, even. Melantha had already experienced far too much heartbreak of her own to find herself bargained away to a human. Nor would Weylind ever sacrifice Jalissa's happiness to something like this.

But Farrendel? Farrendel was illegitimate. He was already disposable, even if Weylind would deny it. He had no happiness left to lose.

Perhaps Weylind had merely meant to avoid confirming that he had a brother, hoping to avoid whatever trap the humans might still be concealing.

King Averett straightened in his chair, jaw tightening. "And I'm not going to marry my sister to an elf without a reciprocating offer from you. Unless your offers of peace weren't genuine?"

Farrendel clenched his fists behind his back, muscles tightening with the renewed tension in the tent. Why were the humans so set on pushing this? Surely if this had been merely a bluff, they would have let it go and tried a different tactic instead to secure whatever trade deal or concessions they actually wanted.

Unless this marriage alliance was what they had wanted all along. Why? What did they have to gain?

Weylind's posture was stiff. Hard, with an edge of his temper showing through. "Your people trespassed into Tarenhiel first. All of Tarenhiel's raids have been in response to your provocation. I believe Escarland should be the first to bend and offer peace as you were the first to harden."

Weylind was giving King Averett an opening to state what he really wanted. This was the moment for the humans to set aside their tricks and lay their intended offer on the table.

King Averett's jaw worked, his shoulders rising and falling. Something in his gaze sparked, as if he, too, fought swelling anger. "As I already stated, I have decried the actions of the few who crossed the border. I'm the one who sent messengers to arrange this talk. I'm the one reaching out for peace first. I believe I have already done my share of bending."

Farrendel's chest knotted hard. The humans were not going to bend. This marriage alliance was what they were after, and they were not going to back down until they got it.

If this was the cost the humans demanded for peace, Weylind would have to pay it. And Weylind was correct. Neither of them was willing to sacrifice their sisters to this.

That meant it would have to be Farrendel.

He clasped his shaking hands behind his back. "Weylind Daresheni. Brother."

Farrendel used his brother's title, meaning Most Honored King, purposefully. He wished to remind Weylind that this decision needed to be made as a king, not just as a brother. A brother might be unwilling to sacrifice a sibling to a marriage alliance, but a king would.

When Weylind turned to him, Farrendel bowed his head, unable to even meet his brother's gaze. "We agreed to accept whatever offer the humans present. This is their offer, and I am willing to accept."

"I will not marry you off to a human any more than I would our sisters." Weylind's jaw hardened. "I will not sacrifice your life like that."

Could Weylind not see that Farrendel's life would be sacrificed either way? Farrendel sacrificed every time he went into battle. If Weylind was willing to risk Farrendel's death on the battlefield, then why not this?

"This is what they want. My life is a small price, in the end." Farrendel clenched his fists tighter behind his back. He was the illegitimate elf prince. It was not as if he ever realistically thought marriage was in his future, much less a happy one. If the humans wanted a marriage, then why not give them an elf prince whose life was worth very little in the end? It would spare lives worth far more than his.

Beside Weylind, Sindrel hunched, as if not wishing to be called upon in this argument between the royal brothers. Next to Farrendel, Iyrinder's posture remained stiff, his gaze scanning the tent as he kept watch while Farrendel was distracted.

"I would not see you miserable." Weylind's expression softened, his gaze searching Farrendel's face. His words held all the hope of a brother who, having a happy and loving marriage to his wife Rheva, wished for the same for his siblings.

What would more misery matter? Yes, it could make his life even harder than it already was. Having his suite of rooms far away from others was the only way he stayed sane after a battle. Having a wife would destroy that one sanctuary.

But what did that matter? He was a weapon to be wielded. He did not have to be sane to kill. Perhaps, it would be better if he was not.

"I will have to either kill them or marry one of them. Please, brother. I have done enough killing." Farrendel hated the way his voice strained over those words. Far too much emotion rising to the surface.

But he would do anything to avoid being drenched in more blood. Even this.

Weylind's posture drooped. "Is this truly what you wish? I will not force you."

Farrendel drew in a long breath, then let it out slowly. Was he being forced? Yes. But that was nothing new. Was this his choice? Yes. Anything was better than a war. Perhaps that was not a very good reason for marriage, but the humans seemed to think nothing of it. It seemed to be a custom of theirs. He let his gaze go hard. "This is my choice."

"Very well." Weylind's tone was not happy, but he faced the human king once again. "He has agreed to marry your princess."

Farrendel had focused on the human princess and thus caught the play of emotion across her face at Weylind's announcement. A widening of her eyes. Shock, maybe? And then, something else that tipped up the corners of her mouth. As if she was happy about this.

She wanted to marry him? Or at least, marry an elf prince. It did something odd in his chest to see her smile.

He could not trust that smile. If she was happy about Weylind's agreement to this arranged marriage, then it had to be yet another human trick. That was all.

And yet, there was her smile. Even as her brother glared first at Weylind, then at Farrendel. "And who is he?"

Weylind's back straightened. "He is my youngest brother, Farrendel Laesornysh."

23

That wiped the smile from the princess's face, replacing it with gaping mouth and far-too-fast breaths.

Farrendel winced. Even the humans had heard of his reputation as Laesornysh. In all likelihood, that was the last he would see her smile.

She let out a long breath, and a smile returned to her face, though even Farrendel could tell this one was far more forced. As King Averett opened his mouth, she gripped his arm, speaking between gritted teeth. "Avie. We need to talk. In private." She sent a far-too-bright smile toward Weylind. "Your Majesty, please excuse my brother and me for a moment."

The princess yanked her brother from his chair and shoved him across the tent to the far side with surprising force.

When they spun to face each other, Farrendel ducked his head. They were not far enough away to prevent him and Weylind from hearing some of what they said. While it was not polite to listen to a conversation, this could give them insight into the humans' plan more than anything else would.

King Averett hissed something so low it was barely audible to Farrendel, using a word with which Farrendel was unfamiliar. The human king continued to speak in a whisper quiet enough Farrendel only caught half of the words, but it seemed the king thought Farrendel might hurt the princess. Was that what the humans thought of elves? That they were cruel?

The princess glanced toward Farrendel and Weylind, then faced her brother with squared shoulders. She spoke loud enough her words were clear. "It's gone too far already. I don't think we can refuse. Nor do I want to."

"You *want* to marry that elf?" King Averett's face twisted, fists clenching.

Farrendel was thinking the same thing, just with less derision. Why was this princess so determined to marry him?

The princess and her brother spoke for several more minutes, but Farrendel could not concentrate enough to make out their words. Not with the way his heart was beating harder in his chest. This human princess was arguing with her brother to marry Farrendel. What made her so determined?

King Averett pulled his sister in close, far closer than elves would in public even with family members.

But whatever they said had the smile back on her face. It bloomed wider as King Averett tweaked her nose. An odd gesture, but it must mean something to human culture.

When she flounced back to her seat, she beamed as if she had been given a gift. Her lips pressed together, twisting as her smile broke through despite her efforts.

King Averett's posture remained stiff as he faced Weylind. "We find a match between my sister and your brother acceptable. I believe her presence with your people will reassure my people that they have an advocate to maintain peaceful relations. Peace will still take time, but I believe it is achievable along this path."

Was the human king hinting at actual peace? Would the humans be satisfied with this marriage alliance and demand nothing more? Farrendel hardly dared hope this marriage alliance could achieve so much. It would be too good to be true, if that were the case.

But there was something in King Averett's tone,

beyond the stiffness. Something that rang like hope, even if it was nothing but Farrendel's wishful thinking.

Yet Weylind must have heard something in King Averett's tone as well, for his posture relaxed a fraction as he nodded. "As do I. If, after a period of six months, your sister's marriage to my brother has sufficiently cooled tensions, I will agree to send one of my sisters for an extended visit to your capital as an ambassador to further peaceful relations."

Farrendel barely kept himself from starting. That was quite the promise that Weylind was laying on the table. It would be risky—perhaps even more risky than this marriage alliance—to send either Melantha or Jalissa into the heart of the humans' capital city.

Yet this promise would buy them time. With this promise dangling in front of them, the humans would hold off any further actions for at least six months. After that, Melantha's or Jalissa's presence as an ambassador might buy them even more time, as well as give them a chance to find out what the humans truly wanted so that they could be better armed when the time came to negotiate for peace yet again.

Farrendel kept his expression neutral, trying to force himself back into the role of guard. Weylind's promise was predicated on the condition that the marriage alliance work. That meant much of the burden would fall on Farrendel's shoulders. Not a comforting thought.

For the rest of the meeting, Farrendel struggled to concentrate. He probably should pay better attention, considering his brother was arranging his wedding. Well, two weddings. The first would be a human style wedding in two days' time—since Weylind did not wish to give the humans any time to plan treachery for the event—and a second, elven wedding when they returned to Estyra.

And all the while, the human princess sat there, that amused smile occasionally breaking onto her face.

Farrendel could not wrap his mind around the fact that she was happy to marry him. Happy. What kind of happiness did she possess that something like this could not shake it?

It did strange things inside his chest. As if, for the first time in years, he felt...hope. Hope that life could be better. Hope that a life with a person like her would not be miserable.

As Farrendel and Weylind left the island late in the afternoon, it occurred to him that he did not even know her name.

THREE

Farrendel braced himself as the boat glided across the water toward the larger ship that would carry them the rest of the way across the river. Sindrel shifted, glancing between them. He, too, would sense the tension dripping from Weylind, although Weylind's expression was impassive.

This would not be a pleasant conversation once they reached the privacy of the ship. Or, if Weylind's self-control lasted that long, the train.

Farrendel swung easily up the side of the ship and landed on deck. He retreated to his designated room before Weylind could corner him. He was not yet ready for that argument.

When the boat docked at the Tarenhieli shore, Weylind fell into step with Farrendel, not allowing him to duck away once they reached the train.

Farrendel suppressed a sigh. He could not avoid this discussion any longer.

When they reached the seating car of the train,

Farrendel planted his feet, clasped his hands behind his back, and waited.

Sindrel scurried into a corner, hovering by the door as if unsure if his king wished to include him in the outburst.

Weylind stalked into the car, slamming the door behind him. He whirled on Sindrel. "Why was a marriage alliance not one of the options for which we planned?"

Sindrel flinched. "It was a common practice among the humans but has been falling out of favor even among them. But the humans know we do not support this practice. I am sorry, my king, that I did not anticipate this tactic."

Weylind tipped his head in a nod. "It was an unexpected tactic. You are dismissed. Please spend tonight researching human marriage alliance customs. I do not wish to be ambushed like that again."

"Yes, Your Majesty." Sindrel nodded and hurried from the train car. Most likely headed for the root system that sent messages across Tarenhiel in order to contact his assistants in the capital of Estyra and ask them to search through the library for information.

Once Sindrel left, Weylind faced Farrendel. "You do not have to do this. We can negotiate for another option."

"This is what the humans want." Farrendel crossed his arms. "If this is what it takes to avoid war, then I must do this."

"I would not have you hurt." Weylind gripped Farrendel's shoulders.

Farrendel suppressed the wry twist to his mouth. Weylind sent Farrendel into battle again and again. This marriage alliance was a little thing. Wiping all expression from his face, he met Weylind's gaze. "She does not seem forced."

"And that makes it worse. This must be a trap. We do not know what the humans have planned that they would want their princess married to you." Weylind stepped back from Farrendel, pacing a few steps down the aisle between the benches. "She could be a spy, sent to get close to the royal family through marriage. Or perhaps she means to assassinate you."

Farrendel huffed out a breath. He held up his hands, releasing his tight grip on his magic. Bolts of magic crackled over his fingers, traveling up his arms. "I can protect myself. I am not about to be assassinated on my wedding night."

He did not sleep deeply enough for that. Even a wife would be hard-pressed to kill him in his sleep.

"She might still be sent to assassinate you. You are the greatest threat to their kingdom." Weylind's mouth thinned.

Farrendel reined in his magic, remembering the look in the princess's eyes. "She is no killer. I would know."

Her eyes were bright. Innocent. Not the eyes of a killer. Not the hard eyes he saw when he looked in a mirror.

"The humans would not consent to a marriage alliance like this unless it was a trick." Weylind paced back toward Farrendel. "All I am asking is that you are cautious. They still see us as the enemy."

Farrendel yanked up his sleeve, revealing the thin scars surrounding his wrist and twisting up his forearm. He gritted his teeth at Weylind's flinch, a sign of the discomfort he was not quick enough to hide. "I can recognize an enemy when I see one."

Weylind frowned as he turned away. "I am not disregarding your judgment."

Farrendel tugged down his sleeve, covering the scars once again. "Then trust me. This is my choice. Besides, it would offend the humans if we refused now. They would see it as an insult to their princess. That would cause the war we wish to avoid."

Weylind's gaze searched Farrendel's face. "All I ask is that you do not grow too attached to her. You love too easily."

Weylind stated it as if loving easily was a bad thing.

For Farrendel, it apparently was. He had formed friendships with some of the children in Ellonahshinel, only to have them turn on him, leaving him with a scar on his cheek from a thrown rock. He had loved the thought of the late elf queen as his mother, only to learn later she had not been his to claim. He loved his siblings, even though he had been separated from Weylind and Melantha for many years growing up.

Perhaps it was a weakness he had inherited from his mother. A mother who had flitted between rich patrons who would pay for her services and call it love. A mother who had abandoned Farrendel the first chance she had to return to the life she had chosen.

A mother Farrendel would have gladly loved, if she had given him the chance.

Farrendel would not be like her. Whatever his weaknesses, he would love meaningfully, and not cheaply.

What would that mean for this arranged marriage? This human princess would be his wife, and that would mean something, no matter how they felt about each other. It would demand his loyalty and a certain amount of attachment. What that would look like, he did not know.

But he could not tell this to Weylind. His brother would fret.

Instead, he sank onto one of the benches, trying to appear relaxed. "I will be careful."

He was not sure why he was being so stubborn about this marriage alliance. It was almost as if he wanted this marriage.

But that could not be it. Just because her smile did something inside his chest did not make him a foolish, young elf falling into an infatuation at first glance. He had fought too many battles to be naïve.

Weylind took a seat across from him, mouth in a tight line. "You are barely a hundred years old. Far too young for marriage."

Farrendel stared back at his brother and did not bother answering. He was a hundred and five. That was full grown, even if most elves waited to marry until full emotional and mental maturity at a hundred and fifty to two hundred. Still, Farrendel was old enough to be sent into battle. That should make him plenty old enough to marry.

When Farrendel did not answer, Weylind's scowl deepened. "We do not even know how old she is. She could be two hundred years older than you."

It was hard to tell with humans. They aged so quickly. But she had not looked to be over two hundred or whatever the human equivalent was. If anything, he would have estimated her age as close to his. One hundred and fifty at the most, which would make her a mere fifty years older. Well within a normal age gap for marriage.

"I do not believe she is that old." Farrendel tried to

force himself to relax against the cushions. As if he was not discussing his marriage to a stranger.

"Even if she is not now, she soon will be as she ages rapidly. Humans have such short lives." Weylind shook his head. "That is why you must not grow attached to her. You will watch her die before you even turn two hundred."

Did Weylind truly think Farrendel would live long enough to see his two hundredth birthday? With the way the incidents at the borders were escalating with both the trolls and the humans, it was highly unlikely Farrendel would survive the upcoming wars.

No, chances were, he was going to die young enough to leave even this human princess a widow.

But he would not say that to Weylind. His brother would be concerned if he knew just how much Farrendel expected—even hoped—to die young.

There was the possibility of an elishina, a heart bond. But that was the kind of far-fetched hope Farrendel was not naïve enough to indulge in, not even now. It was enough to hope that her smiles were something more than a façade for a scheming human bent on killing him in his sleep.

Farrendel shrugged, forcing his tone to remain even. "It will be an arranged marriage. I suspect she will wish to avoid me as much as I wish to avoid her. Attachment should not be an issue. As long as she is cared for well enough to satisfy King Averett and uphold our end of this marriage alliance, that is all that matters."

It sounded like a miserable marriage. Nothing like the marriage Weylind had with Rheva. But what other choice did Farrendel have?

As he had told Weylind, he would either have to

marry her or he would have to kill the Escarlish royal family in the subsequent war. War or marriage. It was that simple.

FARRENDEL WAS NOT sure why his stomach was tight, his heart pounding as he followed Weylind from the boat up the slight rise of Linder Island to the tent that had been left set up overnight. Almost as if he was eager to see the human princess again. Perhaps because he only had today to attempt to talk with her before their wedding on the morrow.

Yet when he stepped into the tent where the humans already gathered, only King Averett and the human diplomat were seated by the table, the princess nowhere in sight.

King Averett stood to greet them, extending his welcome to Farrendel as well as Weylind this time. Was this because he now knew Farrendel was Weylind's brother or because he was soon to marry King Averett's sister?

King Averett held out several sheets of paper. "My diplomat and I spent the evening coming up with a list of human wedding customs you will need to know, along with the marriage vows to memorize."

Weylind moved, as if to reach for them, but Farrendel stretched past him and took the papers first. Yesterday, he had been content to let his brother negotiate the details. But this was Farrendel's wedding. He could not allow Weylind to act as intermediary the entire time.

He scanned the papers. He would need to sit down and study this further as it appeared to be a full outline of a human marriage ceremony. For now, he could quickly search for any issues that would need to be discussed with King Averett before any more planning was completed.

"Do you have any questions?" King Averett's eyes were hard as he all but glared at Farrendel. Why he was so angry about this, Farrendel could not guess. The humans were the ones who had pushed for this alliance.

What questions did he have? He swallowed, his heart beating faster. He had spoken in front of this meeting yesterday. He could do it again.

Use your words, Farrendel. How often had his tutors admonished him to speak up? He did not have trouble speaking with his family, but with others, the words lodged in his throat. The more he cared about their opinion, the more the words stuck.

Yesterday, it had been easier to speak. King Averett had been an enemy, nothing more.

Today, the human king was Farrendel's future brother-in-law.

Farrendel drew in a deep breath and forced the words out. "What is her name?"

King Averett blinked. "Her name?" When Farrendel stared back, King Averett shook his head. "I suppose I didn't properly introduce her, did I? My sister is Princess Elspeth, though she prefers the nickname Essie."

Elspeth. Farrendel let the name sink in, fitting it to her face. Essie.

While Weylind and King Averett settled back into negotiating the particulars of the treaty, Farrendel stood behind Weylind and divided his attention between watching for trouble and studying the pieces of paper.

The human marriage ceremony seemed straightforward enough, though with much more hand-holding than elves would ever do in public. At least very few elves would be in attendance to find such a public display embarrassing.

Except that...Farrendel frowned as he re-read the end of the ceremony. That could not be right. Surely the humans did not do something like kiss in front of a large gathering. That was highly scandalous. Such things were for a couple alone. Not to be gawked at by witnesses.

He tapped Weylind's shoulder. When Weylind glanced up, Farrendel held out the paper and pointed at the section.

Weylind read it, then faced King Averett, set the paper on the table, and pointed at the section that stated the bride and groom would kiss in front of the entire gathering. "This is unacceptable."

King Averett frowned, read the words, then scowled. "You're right. I'm not sure how that ended up included. It's part of a traditional ceremony, but not necessary for a wedding to be legally binding." He took his pen and scratched a line through that section. "Plan on skipping that part of the ceremony."

Farrendel held back his sigh of relief as he reclaimed the paper. The rest of the ceremony seemed doable.

At the next lull in the conversation, he swallowed and forced himself to ask another question. "What manner of attire is expected?"

Elves wore specific clothing for a wedding due to what their ceremony entailed. But Farrendel had not seen anything in the human wedding that would necessitate a particular style.

King Averett glanced at him. "It is usually fancy, ball-room style clothing, though the bride's dress is more important than the groom's attire." When Farrendel continued to stare at him, King Averett gestured. "What you're wearing now is fine."

Farrendel nodded. He had an even fancier tunic and trousers with him in case it was needed for any formal ceremony as part of the treaty signing. As his wedding was the formal ceremony, he might as well wear it then.

When it was finally time to return to their train that evening, Farrendel retreated to his private train car, not wishing for yet another argument with Weylind, and retrieved a box from one of the shelves beneath the windows.

Inside the box lay his circlet, a silver band formed from twining leaves and branches. Like his ceremonial tunic, he had taken the crown in case something more formal was necessary.

Also in the box lay several rings that matched the crown. Even though many among the elven court favored wearing rings for ornamentation, Farrendel had never worn them, as he did not like the constriction of rings on his fingers or how they rubbed against the hilts of his swords.

But they would serve a purpose now. Apparently, it was rather important in a human ceremony that the groom gift a ring to the bride.

What size was Princess Elspeth's finger? He closed his eyes. Small, if he remembered right. As elven fingers tended to be long and slim, any number of these rings should fit her.

He chose a simple band that matched the crown but did not have some of the heavier bands or flourishes of some of the other rings. It seemed the safest choice.

If he had any conceptions about what his marriage

would be like, this was not it. He had never expected he would marry, much less marry a complete stranger. A human, no less.

His reputation, forever damaged thanks to his illegitimate birth, would be even more damaged because of this. One more flaw for an already flawed elf prince.

He could perhaps redeem himself in the eyes of the court if he made it clear how unwilling he was in the match. How it was merely to appease the humans and nothing more.

And yet, when he thought of Princess Elspeth's smile, he could not comprehend ignoring her like that.

Weylind was right. Farrendel was already growing too attached to her. He knew nothing about her besides her smile and her name, and yet here he was contemplating choosing her over the honor before the elven court that he had worked his whole life to gain.

Never trust a human bargain. That was the warning. But what about a human's smile?

CHAPTER

FOUR

arrendel straightened his circlet one last time,
feeling the sway in the deck beneath his feet as
the ship gently docked on the Escarlish shore.
He faced the mirror in his cabin before he turned away.

This would be the first time an elven king had peace-
fully stepped foot on Escarlish soil in hundreds of years.
Weylind never had, though he thought their father might
have early in his reign before Escarland had grown into
the powerful nation it was now and the current tensions
had arisen. Their grandmother Leyleira would know. She
occasionally told stories of a time when humans and elves
were allies, rather than enemies.

It would be the first time in living memory for the
humans. A momentous occasion.

Unless it was a trap.

When King Averett had insisted the human-style
wedding be held on the Escarlish shore, Weylind had
reluctantly agreed. But he had warned Farrendel to stay
alert. Getting the elf king into an Escarlish outpost where

he could be surrounded by hundreds of soldiers and ambushed could be the entire reason the humans had pushed for this marriage alliance, never mind the peace treaty they had so eagerly signed that morning.

Alliance or ambush? Which would it be?

Farrendel did not wear his swords. It did not seem appropriate to be so obtrusively armed at his wedding. Instead, he had hidden knives in his boots, up his sleeves, beneath his tunic between his shoulder blades, and at the small of his back.

If this was an ambush, it would be up to him to extricate his brother safely. It would not matter how many Escarlish soldiers he killed. This ceremonial tunic would end the day as blood-spattered rags.

His stomach churned. He needed this to be anything other than an ambush.

Yet that would mean he was really getting married today. Worse, he would have to get married all over again tomorrow in Estyra. Two ceremonies. Two large gatherings filled with people staring at him. Two events where he would be expected to talk in front of people.

One bride who was a total stranger.

His stomach twisted harder. Alliance or ambush. Either way, he just wanted it over.

When he left his stateroom on the boat, he joined Weylind, Iyrinder, and Sindrel on the main deck. If they had known there would be an event like this held on Escarland's shore, they would have brought more warriors with them.

But most of the warriors were still at the border with Kostaria, dealing with the last of the raiding trolls, and the rest were needed in Estyra guarding the royal family. If something went wrong today, it was important Farrendel's nephew Ryfon remained alive and well to assume the throne with Weylind's wife Rheva there to be the queen mother and advisor.

Farrendel would do everything in his power to prevent that. Ryfon was about the same age Farrendel had been when he had lost his father. That was a tragedy he would not see repeated for another generation.

Nor was Ryfon nearly as ready as Weylind had been when Weylind took the throne. Thanks to their father all but abdicating the throne first in his grief at the loss of his wife, then to raise Farrendel, Weylind had essentially been ruling as king a hundred years before the crown officially became his.

A gangplank was lowered, and Weylind led the way onto the dock. There, a contingent of four Escarlish soldiers met them.

A tall man with short brown hair and a trimmed beard —the human male facial hair Farrendel had heard about but never seen up close—stepped forward. His gaze studied Farrendel for a moment before focusing on Weylind. He gave a half-bow. "I am Prince Julien of Escarland, one of King Averett's younger brothers. We are your escort, Your Majesty."

Weylind tipped his head in acknowledgment. Then they were following Prince Julien and the Escarlish soldiers up an embankment from the river toward the wooden-walled outpost built on a hill overlooking the river.

Farrendel resisted the urge to swipe his palms on his trousers. Once they stepped inside those walls, they would be at the mercy of the Escarlish soldiers, or so the Escarlish might assume.

At least the outpost was made of wood. Wood gave

them an advantage. Weylind could transform the dead logs into living branches, turning the humans' fort against them. And if Farrendel let his magic burst in all its uncontrollable fury, he could level the place in a few seconds.

But that would mean killing every Escarlish man and woman inside, including Princess Elspeth and her joyful smile.

He needed this to be a wedding and not an ambush. He was not sure he could hold on to his sanity if he were forced to kill the person he had thought he was going to marry, for all that she was a stranger.

The doors to the outpost were wide open, though Escarlish soldiers stood beside the gates and on the wall top, muskets on their shoulders as they patrolled. Farrendel kept his head high, even as he felt the weight of their gazes scrutinizing him.

Prince Julien led them to a long building. Faint strains of music from some stringed instrument echoed from inside. "This is the dining hall, though it has been cleared for the event. I believe the guests have already gathered."

Guests? Or soldiers waiting to spring a trap?

King Averett met them at the door. His gaze flicked over Farrendel before he grimaced and nodded. "Good. You're here. Julien, get the ceremony started while I fetch Essie."

The human king sounded like he was at a funeral rather than a wedding. What did it mean? Was it because he was planning an ambush? Or because he was marrying his sister to an elf?

Prince Julien pushed open the door and led the way inside. It must have been some kind of signal, for the music changed from lilting to something more ponderous and ceremonial. Prince Julien spoke in a lowered tone.

"We might as well enter as a group. Prince Farrendel, you'll stay standing at the end of the aisle while the rest of us take our seats in the front row."

Farrendel nodded. That part was not unlike elven weddings. Even the part of the bride making a grand entrance was similar. It made him wonder just how much human and elven customs had once influenced each other in the past.

Weylind and Prince Julien led the way, with Farrendel following. Sindrel and Iyrinder dropped to walk behind him. As they strode down the aisle formed out of many long benches, Farrendel scanned the crowd as best he could without turning his head. What appeared to be a few noblemen and women sat in the rows near the front while the rest of the rows were filled with men in Escarlish uniforms.

A human woman wearing a crown sat all alone in the front row, her red hair showing just a few lighter streaks where it was going a white-gray as she aged. As the hair was similar enough to Princess Elspeth's, she must be some relation to the princess, but Farrendel did not dare make any guesses. Humans aged so differently, he was not sure how old the woman was.

It was another sign that this was a genuine wedding. Surely the humans would not have gathered their nobles and even more of their women, especially not one of their royalty, if this was an elaborate trap to kill Weylind.

At the front, Farrendel took his place by a white-haired man, the human officiant mentioned in the description of the ceremony he had memorized.

Prince Julien took the seat next to the older human woman and directed Weylind, Sindrel, and Iyrinder to the seats in the front row on the other side of the aisle. The row behind Weylind had been left empty, giving Weylind's back some protection from the Escarlish nobles sitting two rows behind him.

Still, Farrendel scanned the room for any sign of trouble. Unless King Averett planned to be personally present for an ambush, this would be a perfect moment for it before Princess Elspeth was supposed to arrive.

The music changed again. Those gathered rose to their feet and turned toward the back of the room.

Princess Elspeth entered the aisle on King Averett's arm, though there was barely room for him beside her due to the volume of her skirts. Farrendel had never seen a dress with such frilly, poofy dimensions before. It boggled the mind that the humans would use that much fabric for a single dress.

He swallowed as he lifted his gaze from Princess Elspeth's dress to her face. Beneath the crown of red curls, her smile was bright, if somewhat strained. Was she nervous? Because of a planned ambush or because she, too, was marrying a stranger?

When she reached the front and he clasped her fingers, they were warm and somewhat sweaty. Yes, she was nervous. He did not know how to reassure her, especially with so many people watching.

As the ceremony began, he divided his attention between listening for his cue, scanning the crowd for trouble, and glancing at her so that she did not feel ignored by her groom at her own wedding.

His chest knotted painfully tight. So many eyes on him. It took all his effort to breathe and keep his magic buried deep.

And Princess Elspeth was staring at him. His skin prickled with the intense focus of her eyes. Was something wrong? Well, more wrong than marrying a stranger?

Perhaps she had noticed his scars. Not many were visible right now, except for the one on his cheek and, if she looked close enough, the faint lines on his neck above the collar of his tunic. Maybe she was as disgusted by them as most elves were.

He pressed his mouth tight against a scowl, and she looked away. Had she noticed his momentary lapse in discipline? He should not allow so much unbridled expression in front of such a large crowd.

When the time came, he managed to remember the vows he had memorized. He slid the ring on her finger when prompted, thankful it appeared to fit well enough. Finally, the human officiant declared them married, and the ceremony was over. No ambush. No massacre caused by his magic. No blood pooling in the aisle and soaking the white of Princess Elspeth's dress.

It was a real wedding. And he was really married.

CHAPTER

FIVE

As soon as the ceremony finished, Farrendel released Princess Elspeth's hands, resisting the urge to rub his palms on his tunic. Such an intimate gesture to perform in front of strangers. Humans were given to such displays of emotion.

As Princess Elspeth's family stepped toward her, Farrendel eased away until he reached the corner. All he wanted to do was bolt out of there. Too many people. Too many potential enemies.

He did not hide well enough. King Averett and Prince Julian tromped up to him, boxing him in.

King Averett crossed his arms. "Tonight, you are going to leave with my sister. We're trusting you that she will come to no harm. Not from you. Not from anyone."

"And if she gets hurt, we will hurt you." Prince Julien also crossed his arms, flexing muscles in his shoulders and biceps. He was as tall as Farrendel, but far bulkier.

Still, neither of them posed that much of a threat to him. Not with his magic.

But he took the warning to heart. Even if King Averett was willing to sacrifice his sister to a marriage alliance to forge peace, he cared for her. He would not take it kindly if something happened to her.

Farrendel's stomach clenched again. If Princess Elspeth was hurt, her brothers would not be happy. This entire peace treaty rested on how well Farrendel took care of this human princess.

He would do his best, but he barely functioned on the days after a battle. How would he manage to keep another person well and happy and everything he was not?

But he nodded. What else could he do? They had a point. He was married to her now. It was a little late to have second thoughts.

That seemed to satisfy them. Enough that they did not hassle him again through the brief supper. Nor did Farrendel spot any other signs of trouble. Perhaps the humans were going to let him, the other elves, and his new wife walk out of here without incident.

When they finished eating, Farrendel stood to the side as Princess Elspeth said farewell to her family, including the older red-haired woman, one last time. They were even doing that human hugging thing. In public. With everybody watching.

Princess Elspeth reached down to pick up a sack set in the corner, but Prince Julien hefted it, marched over to Farrendel, and shoved it at him. "You're her husband now. Be a gentleman and carry Essie's things."

For a moment, all Farrendel could do was stare. Surely this was not all of her things. She was a princess. She would not travel with her personal effects stuffed into a sack.

Prince Julien shoved it at him again, and Farrendel quickly took it. It was heavier than it looked. What was in here?

No matter. Time to leave. Finally. He held his arm out to Princess Elspeth. Instead of resting her hand on his arm, she wrapped her hand around his elbow. He stared at her hand, half-hoping she would move it to his forearm as an elf would if he stared at it long enough.

She did not. And it would take too many words to explain.

Straightening his shoulders, he strode after Weylind, trying not to trip as Princess Elspeth's massive skirt kept bumping into him. He had to pause at the door as she wedged her skirt through. If it was such a cumbersome thing, why did she wear it?

Human fashions were strange and impractical. Hopefully she did not intend to wear such dresses in Estyra. A dress like that would be incompatible with the way the bridges and pathways were designed.

But…he sneaked a glance at the princess at his side as they navigated down the hill toward the wharf. If she wished to cling to the fashions of her homeland, he would not tell her otherwise. Leaving everything she had ever known must be hard enough on her as it was. He would not force her to give up her manner of dress, her customs, or change herself.

This was an arranged marriage. In the end, they might discover they could barely tolerate each other and would hold each other at a distance.

But she was his wife, however it had come about. That meant he owed her a certain level of caring, however much Weylind counseled against it.

Farrendel had two examples in his parents. He had his

mother, who had turned her back on him for her own convenience. Weylind did not yet see that this was exactly what Farrendel would be doing if he ignored Princess Elspeth.

Then there was Farrendel's father. He could have avoided scandal. He could have sent Farrendel away to be raised elsewhere, never truly acknowledged or a part of the family. That would have been the far easier course of action.

Instead, Dacha had taken responsibility and claimed Farrendel as his own. He had faced the scandal head-on and had never backed down when he was challenged about making Farrendel a full member of the royal family.

And when he had died, Weylind had followed his example and had not sent Farrendel away as many in the court had suggested. To this day, he introduced Farrendel as his brother without hesitation, taking the scandal upon himself even though he carried none of the blame.

That was the example Farrendel wanted to follow. That was the kind of choice he wanted to make. The circumstances of this marriage were out of his control, but he could choose how he reacted to them. That started with caring for Princess Elspeth's wellbeing the best he knew how.

If he could manage it. All the fighting and killing left him so hollow. So broken. What part of himself could he give her when it felt like it took all his strength to just hold himself together?

As they strolled up the gangplank onto the ship, Princess Elspeth turned and waved her arm wildly. It must have been some kind of human farewell custom, for her family, now lined up at the end of the dock, waved their hands back, though less boisterously than the princess did.

As soon as the gangplank was pulled onto the ship, Princess Elspeth grabbed her sack of belongings from him, turning to face him with a wide smile on her face. "Unless you're fine with me stumbling around in this fancy dress all night, is there any place I can change aboard this vessel? There should be time enough before we reach the other side."

Farrendel blinked back at her. He had not mentally prepared for what he should do now. Should he take her to his stateroom? Or would she find that presumptuous? Would she rather have her own stateroom? But the only unoccupied ones were deeper in the ship, and he was not sure her dress would fit down the passageway.

He glanced away from her, trying to buy himself time to think. Sindrel and Iyrinder scurried past, heads down, as if fleeing for their lives.

Weylind met his gaze then gestured from Farrendel to Princess Elspeth. Even he appeared bewildered, and he was the one with experience being married. Should not he be the one offering wisdom right now?

Farrendel suppressed a sigh. Weylind was right. He could not rely on others to do this for him. If he had not been prepared to take on the responsibility of caring for her, then he should not have agreed to this marriage.

With a shake of her head and a smile far too wide to be anything but forced, Princess Elspeth spun on her heels and marched away from him. "Never mind. I'll just explore and find something."

Had he offended her with his silence? Words. He needed to use his words. If only he could get his brain and his tongue to cooperate. Both seemed to be frozen at the moment.

He forced himself to catch up to her, then pass her. "This way."

He would take her to his stateroom. It made the most logical sense. He would give her plenty of space once there.

With a plan in place, he led her to the hatch nearest his stateroom in the stern. He went down first, then stood back as she wiggled and maneuvered and wedged her dress through the opening. He would have helped, but he was not sure what she would consider help and what she would consider inappropriate. The last thing he wanted to do was offend her when they had been married all of a few hours.

His room was the second one on the passageway, just past Weylind's. He opened the door, then stood back to let her enter first. After another round of wiggling, she forced her dress inside.

Beneath them, the ship picked up speed as it pulled away from the wharf. Should he just close the door and leave? Would she want him to guard the door? Was there anything else she needed?

She spun back toward him. "What is powering the ship? Is it magic?"

The ship? Why was she asking about the ship's propulsion? He managed to dredge up the answer. "Yes."

She kept staring at him, as if waiting for something. What else did she want? Or need? What was she expecting him to do now?

He stayed in the doorway, not wanting to step into the room and crowd her nor leave and abandon her.

With a shrug, she swept her gaze around the room. He

was not sure what she thought of it. It was a standard cabin with a bed grown into the wall and his clothes neatly laid on the shelves. He did not see anything he had left out of place.

"This is a beautiful cabin. It looks like someone is staying here." Her eyebrows furrowed as she glanced over her shoulder at him.

No avoiding it now. He could not meet her gaze. "It is mine."

What would she think, him bringing her here? He did not mean anything by it besides giving her a private place to change. Nothing more. They were strangers, and he would demand nothing from her.

Space. She needed space. And he needed it. Desperately.

The moment she glanced away from him, he backed the rest of the way out of the doorway and shut the door swiftly and silently, leaning against it.

His hands were shaking. He clenched them to stop the trembling. Admit it. He was downright terrified of that human princess in the room behind him. Terrified he would do or say the wrong thing. Terrified he would hurt her and thereby hurt the alliance. Worried he would not be enough.

"Brother?" Weylind's voice drifted through the hatchway.

Farrendel quickly straightened and wiped all emotion from his face. "Did you require something?"

Weylind dropped down the ladder and into the passageway. "No."

That meant Weylind was checking to make sure Farrendel was all right. As much as he appreciated it,

Farrendel gritted his teeth against the constant hovering. He was fine. He would deal with this.

Farrendel pushed from the door and strode closer to Weylind. "I am fine."

He had to be. It was not Weylind's job to piece him back together if he was not.

Weylind paced across the passageway. "You have already sacrificed greatly for Tarenhiel. You are not alone in this. I will stand by you. And if she turns out to be a spy or an assassin sent by the humans…"

"She is not." Farrendel was certain she was no assassin. He could not be so certain that she was not a spy, but it would not matter. The humans would quickly learn they had married their princess to the wrong elf if they had wanted access to the upper echelons of elven politics. Besides fending off raids when called upon, Farrendel kept to himself and stayed out of the life of the elven court as much as possible.

Weylind scowled. "Do not be so trusting."

Farrendel nearly huffed a frustrated breath on that one. Perhaps he should have learned his lesson by now. He had the scars to prove the dangers of being too trusting, too naïve. But he could not bring himself to treat her as an enemy instead of a wife. "I am not."

The door to Farrendel's room opened and shut with a click.

Bracing himself, he turned to his wife. Blinked. Blinked again. Tried to make sense of what he was seeing.

She was wearing his clothes. His plain, green tunic sagged from her shoulders while the sleeves of his shirt hung over her hands, even though she had rolled up the ends. She wore one of his trousers underneath with a pair of low boots that must belong to her since that was the only part of her ensemble that was not his. Her vibrant red hair had been taken down from its style on the top of her head to lie down her back, vivid against the green of the tunic.

She was the most adorable sight he had ever seen.

His mouth dried, his heart pounded harder. Something flipped in his chest, painful and tight.

"Those are mine." He clamped his mouth shut. Had he really just blurted that out loud? In Escarlish? What was wrong with him?

She faced him, her eyes a blue-green. "I hope you don't mind if I borrow them. I don't have any elven clothes yet, and these are much more practical for scrambling around boats and whatever else we are going to do for the next part of the journey to Estyra. You don't mind if I borrow it, do you?"

Had she even paused for a breath for that entire paragraph? He was not sure if he should be bewildered at all those words strung together or impressed at her lung function. What was he supposed to say to that?

Next to him, Weylind eyed him and raised an eyebrow, as if, for all his misgivings about this marriage, he found it highly entertaining that Farrendel would find himself stuck with a human who could talk at such a rapid rate.

What was Farrendel supposed to do when she stood there wearing his clothes and giving him such a wide-eyed innocent look? Finally, he managed to shake his head.

Princess Elspeth let out a small huff, but her mouth quirked into a smile. "I will take that as a no, you don't have a problem with me borrowing your clothes. I'm sorry I left your room in a mess. I didn't know what to do with my wedding dress. I like it. It made me feel like the princess I am. But it will hardly be in style in Estyra."

Words. He needed words. Farrendel swallowed, and it took all his concentration to remember how to breathe normally.

She gave a shrug and waved over her shoulder. "Anyway, your room is available. If you want to change into your other tunic. I'm sorry I took this one." She paused, glanced at him, and shifted. "What am I supposed to call you? Farrendel? Or do you prefer Laesornysh? Do elves have nicknames? Can I call you Farren?"

Farren? He struggled not to let his disgust show on his face. Thankfully, the emotion gave him the words he needed. "Farrendel is fine."

"All right." She rocked on her heels, her smile dimming after a moment. "So am I allowed on deck? I'd love to see the Tarenhieli shore as it approaches. It always looks so mysterious from across the river, just a smudge of green trees. If you don't mind me wandering around alone, you don't have to escort me. You probably want to change, and I can find my way to the bow of a boat."

While he did not want to spend the night sleeping in these clothes, he did not have to change yet. She had taken the clothes he had intended to sleep in that night, but he had others on the train. He traveled with enough clothes that he would not run out if a few became too blood-spattered to be salvageable.

But he could not form the words to tell her that. Instead, he held out his arm to her. With a shrug, she took his elbow again and trotted at his side to the ladder, which she scrambled up without any prompting.

On deck, she hurried to the bow and leaned on the rail. The nighttime breeze toyed with strands of her red hair, and Farrendel found himself watching her more than the shoreline of his homeland drawing closer.

"How are we going to travel to Estyra? Do you elves have trains? You must. You have a steamboat, after all. Well, not really a steamboat since it is powered by magic. But you do have your own version of technology. How long will it take to get to Estyra?"

How many of those questions did she expect him to answer? He swayed in time to the motion of the boat. Exhaustion was beginning to seep into his muscles, resting heavy and gritty on his eyelids. It had been an early morning and a long day. How did she have so much energy this late into the evening?

She sighed and sagged against the rail, her smile dimming. "Never mind. Guess I'll find out myself."

What had he done to make her stop smiling? And what did he have to do to bring her smile back?

"We have trains." Everything in him wanted to turn and run. Why could he not say something intelligent when he was around her?

"Oh, good. That will make things easier." She yawned, covering her mouth with a hand.

So she was tired. Was all this chatter her way of hiding her tiredness?

His own tiredness weighed on his shoulders and eyelids. In normal circumstances, he would have retired for the night long before this.

"You can call me Essie, by the way. I like it so much better than Elspeth. But Elspeth was my grandmother's name, and I heard she was a nice person, so I am honored to carry her name, even if I prefer my nickname." Somehow she managed to say all that even while yawning yet again.

The shortened name Essie did seem to suit her better than Elspeth did. Yet he struggled to get his mind around the concept of shortening names like that. Did it not diminish the meaning behind it? As his name meant fair one or, more properly translated, he of the fair hair, shortening his name to Farren would be like calling him just by his hair color. He was not sure of the Escarlish equivalent, but it would be something like Blondie. Or calling her Red.

Her gaze flicked to him before focusing on the nearing trees. Her mouth pressed into a thin line, the smile disappearing from her eyes.

Right. He had been too busy thinking to manage a response to her. What was she expecting him to say?

The ship eased against the wharf. The gangplank was lowered, and Farrendel held out his arm for Princess Elspeth. She once again gripped his elbow instead of resting her hand on the top of his forearm, but he was far too tired to attempt to explain.

He led the princess on the short walk from the wharf to the train. A few servants passed them going the other direction to gather the things from the ship to load onto the train. Farrendel stopped one of them and asked the servant to load Princess Elspeth's things into Farrendel's train car.

To give the servants time to load the car, Farrendel led Princess Elspeth to the seating car. She climbed inside, gazing about with wide eyes and a smile in place. When she spotted the benches, she plopped onto one and stretched out. "Wake me up when we get there."

Wait, what? Farrendel stared at her as she curled onto the bench. Did she intend to sleep there? He was supposed to be the one sleeping on a bench, not her.

He had planned to show her to his sleeping car and give her the bed. The car had locking doors, so she would have felt safe while he slept out here.

And yet, here she was, curling up on a bench without even waiting to be shown around. Did humans not have sleeping cars and proper beds on their trains? Rather barbaric, if that was the case.

Her shoulders already rose and fell in sleep. How did she manage to go from chattering nonstop to asleep within moments?

She was so innocently naïve. She did not fear what would happen if she slept with enemies around her. She was not afraid of waking up alone in the dark with stone threaded beneath her skin, pinned to the floor and helpless.

She was trusting, so very trusting. Without a fear that she could be hurt as she slept.

Should Farrendel carry her to the sleeping car? It would be more comfortable for her, yet he did not wish to touch her without her permission, not even for something as innocent as that.

Weylind entered the train, then glanced down at Princess Elspeth, raising an eyebrow.

Farrendel shifted. "She seemed to wish to sleep here."

Weylind gave a small shrug. "Then let her. You should get a good night of rest. It will be a long day tomorrow as well."

Another long day, when he got married yet again.

He hesitated. There were few others on the train. She was safe.

Yet he could not leave her alone. It was still his job to make sure she was safe. He might not be able to gift her with his heart as ought to be the case in a marriage, but he could gift her this. While she was in Tarenhiel, she would never, ever have to fear for her safety. Not from him, not from any elf.

Farrendel eased onto the bench across from Princess Elspeth. "I will stay here."

Weylind shook his head and huffed, as if he wanted to mutter under his breath about not getting attached to tricky, short-lived humans. He left the seating car, headed for his private train car.

Farrendel stretched out on the bench, though he avoided looking at Princess Elspeth. She did not need him to stare at her while she slept.

Moments later, Weylind returned, carrying pillows and blankets. He set the mound on the bench next to Farrendel.

"Linshi." Farrendel sat up and reached for the blankets. Weylind had brought two blankets and two pillows, probably knowing Farrendel would give up his to Princess Elspeth if Weylind brought only one set.

"Rest well." Weylind nodded and left.

Farrendel spread a blanket over the princess without touching her, then tucked the pillow next to her head. Perhaps she would shift enough to grab it in her sleep.

He made a mental note to wake before she did and reclaim the blanket and pillow in the morning. He had no wish to have her wake in a state of panic when she realized items were there that had not been there when she had fallen asleep.

Then, he curled on the bench across from her, though it took hours for him to drift into a light sleep. He did not dare sleep too deeply. The last thing he wanted to do was suffer a nightmare. That would surely scare her and undo all his efforts to guard her while she slept.

SIX

Farrendel's stomach sank as he strolled through Estyra with Princess Elspeth on his arm, her hand on his forearm in the proper elven custom this time. How was his family going to react to this?

Princess Elspeth gazed about with wide eyes, smiling. At least she did not appear to find her new home unpleasant. He was not sure why it was so important to him that she like it here. As Weylind was forever reminding him, Farrendel could not hang too many hopes on this marriage. He should not get attached.

As the path turned and the forest opened in front of them to the grassy stretch surrounding Ellonahshinel, Princess Elspeth caught her breath and leaned into him, her fingers tightening on his arm. Her steps turned into almost a bounce, as if she dearly wanted to ask a question but was restraining herself.

And, somehow, her excitement made him want to answer the questions she had not asked. "Ellonahshinel."

It was easier to keep talking if he kept his gaze focused on the tree palace ahead of them. Looking at people when he talked tied his tongue. "In your language, it means Heart of the Forest."

She nodded and grinned. As if she was happy to be here.

They ascended the stairs up the spreading roots of Ellonahshinel and entered the formal entry hall. There, his family was lined up, waiting.

Farrendel swallowed and braced himself for their reaction. Weylind had sent a message letting them know Farrendel was bringing a human bride back to Estyra. But that did not mean they would be mentally prepared for such a thing.

As their gazes flicked from Farrendel to Princess Elspeth, their jaws tightened. Eyes hardened.

This was not going to go well.

After an awkward moment, Weylind's wife Rheva stepped forward, and Weylind rested his hands on her shoulders, murmuring too low for anyone else to hear. Farrendel told himself he was not jealous of the warmth in Rheva's eyes or the softness that eased Weylind's features when he looked at his wife.

After Rheva stepped back, Weylind greeted Ryfon and Brina, his son and daughter. Then Weylind moved to Melantha and Jalissa.

Farrendel waited, Princess Elspeth at his side, as everyone turned in their direction. He struggled to find the words to tell them...something. Anything.

Weylind glanced at him and must have seen his hesitation. He gestured to Farrendel and Princess Elspeth. "This is Princess Elspeth of Escarland, Farrendel's wife."

"I cannot believe you really allowed those humans to marry their princess to him." Melantha clenched her fists.

"It was the condition the humans placed on the treaty." Weylind's shoulders slumped as he glanced at Farrendel. As if he felt he had failed in some way.

"How could you let him marry a human? The court already scorns him. This will only make it worse. The last thing this family needs is another scandal." Melantha jabbed her finger first at Farrendel, then at Princess Elspeth, before finishing by spinning to Weylind. "We do not have to go through with this. Especially not a public wedding."

Farrendel stepped in front of Princess Elspeth to shield her from his family. "Melantha, this is my choice. We need peace. She is the way to get it. Besides, we are already married, and Tarenhiel honors Escarlish marriages as binding. The wedding here is merely to ensure there is no doubt, and so that my family can attend. Now, will you aid me or not?"

Melantha glared and crossed her arms. Still not happy whatsoever.

Jalissa let out a sigh and met his gaze. "Is this truly what you want?"

Melantha huffed and swiveled her gaze to the ceiling for a moment. "He was forced to marry her for a treaty. Of course this is not what he wants."

Farrendel glared back and did not try to correct her. He was not sure how to put a retort into words. Yes, he had been forced to marry Princess Elspeth. But he had done it willingly. Because marrying her was far better than a war. And, perhaps, because her smile did something inside his chest that felt almost like happiness.

"What is done is done." Rheva's calm voice cut through the tension. She held herself with dignity, as a queen of the elves. "Right now, we need to focus on arranging a wedding fit for our brother. Now, Farrendel, please introduce us to your bride."

Farrendel would never take Weylind's wife for granted. She had married into the family, knowing she would someday become the queen of the elves. Yet, within a few decades of marriage, she weathered the loss of the late elf queen and the scandal of Farrendel's birth and acknowledgment. Less than a hundred years later, she found herself queen far sooner than she should have when Farrendel's father was killed.

She could have scorned Farrendel. His existence had made her life far harder than it should have been. Yet she had stuck by Weylind—and thus Farrendel—unfailingly.

Farrendel introduced each of his family members to Princess Elspeth. Then he gestured to her. "And this is Princess Elspeth Amirah."

While Farrendel did not think she understood elvish, she must have understood enough. Because she smiled. "But you can call me Essie."

The same shortened name her brother had called her. What was this human custom of a short name? Did it have any deeper meaning?

Melantha wrinkled her nose and opened her mouth as if about to say something.

Farrendel held up a hand. He did not want to hear any more. "Please, isciena."

"Fine. If this is what you want, I will plan the wedding." Melantha spun on her heel and swept from the room.

Weylind glanced at Rheva, something passing between them, before he turned back to Farrendel. "Rheva will aid her, and I will ensure the court knows this will be a wedding fit for a prince of the elves."

In other words, Weylind would make sure the court knew they could not afford to shun this wedding. Not if they wanted to avoid bringing upon themselves the displeasure of their king.

Once Weylind, Rheva, Ryfon, and Brina left, Farrendel turned to Princess Elspeth. She peered at him with trusting eyes that appeared greener in the green depths of the forest. Standing this close to her, he could see the smattering of freckles across her cheeks. A wisp of her red hair fell across her forehead. He had to take a deep breath to clear his thoughts. "The wedding will be tonight."

Her eyes widened. Perhaps he should have thought of a better way to deliver that news.

"Rheva and Melantha have agreed to arrange it while Jalissa will help you prepare." Farrendel gave Princess Elspeth a nudge toward Jalissa. With his hand on her back, he felt her deep breath, as if bracing herself.

How frightened was she? It was hard to tell past her ever-present smiles. If only he could reassure her that she was safe here. But she would likely not believe him if he did.

Farrendel started for the door, but he paused next to Jalissa, glancing back to Princess Elspeth. He had much to accomplish, but he found himself strangely reluctant to leave her. "Look after her."

"I will, shashon." Jalissa patted his arm, her smile soft. She did not ask why he was doing this, though he could see she wanted to.

Farrendel could trust Jalissa with Princess Elspeth. She was far less hardened and bitter than Melantha.

With one last glance at Princess Elspeth, Farrendel turned and strolled from the room. He wound his way across the branches, farther and farther from the bustle of the center of the tree, until he reached the branch that contained his rooms. The peace and quiet here settled into his mind and heart.

Except...he grimaced. Three servants were approaching, one male and two female. One carried the sack of Princess Elspeth's belongings, one carried Farrendel's travel bag, and the last could barely see over the puffy white mound of fabric she hugged as she tried to keep all the fabric from tripping her.

"Amir, where would you like the amirah's things?" The female servant carrying Princess Elspeth's sack of belongings halted before Farrendel.

The male servant simply dropped Farrendel's travel case on the porch of the main room, nodded to Farrendel, and left. Farrendel nodded in return. The servants knew his quirks, though they probably did not know the reason he barred servants from so much as stepping foot in his rooms.

This was his sanctuary free of other people. The one place he could relax.

Princess Elspeth would change that. His sanctuary here would no longer have the peace and quiet it once did.

The female servants were still standing there, waiting.

"Put her things in the first guest bedroom." Surely she was not expecting to move into his room. Hopefully she would be content to keep to herself on her branch while he stayed on his.

As the female servant edged past him, Farrendel had to lean back to give room for the servant with the large white wedding gown.

Princess Elspeth had said something about how she loved that dress. Today would be strange enough for her. Perhaps she should have this piece of her homeland with her.

"Wait." Farrendel swallowed. He could not meet the servant's gaze as he gathered his thoughts into words. "Please take this dress to the seamstress. Ask her to remake it in our style for the princess's wedding dress."

The servant blinked at him for a moment, probably thinking him addled for asking the seamstress to turn that monstrosity of fabric into something presentable. But then she nodded. "Very well, amir."

The tightness in his shoulders did not relax until both servants had left, toting the frothy white wedding dress between them.

He crossed the porch and entered the main room of his living quarters. The countertop and cupboards in the kitchen section remained as empty and spotless as he had left them. To the other side, cushions covered the floor, for relaxing. Not that Farrendel spent much time lounging.

Instead of entering his room, he took the middle doorway and climbed the stairway formed out of the branch up to the guest bedroom perched higher on the branch. A small porch ringed the room grown into the tree. Twigs and leaves grew from the walls and the porch posts.

What would Princess Elspeth think when she saw it? He was unsure what human dwellings looked like, though if they were anything like the fort by the river, they were large and square and solid. Not like the airy and open elven homes.

He stepped inside. The place was clean, at least. The servants had placed Princess Elspeth's things on the clothing shelves and made the bed. Farrendel took a moment to check the attached water closet. It was stocked with soap, shampoo, and conditioner on the chance he ever had a guest who needed them. As he had never had guests, they had never been used.

Perhaps he could take Princess Elspeth to visit Illyna, a former warrior and friend of his who ran her own shop, to pick out new shampoo and conditioner. It would give them something to do, at least.

This place was as ready for her as he could make it.

He returned to the main room and stared for far too long at his luggage sitting in the middle of the floor.

He needed to get ready for his wedding. Again. He had already married her once, yet somehow this time seemed more momentous. Even though he had much to do before the wedding, he found himself standing there paralyzed.

A knock came on his door, snapping him out of his paralysis. He bit back his urge to tell the person there to leave. On this day, he would most likely have to bear all sorts of intrusions into his sanctuary.

He strode to the door and opened it. As soon as he did, he was thankful he had held back his order to leave.

His grandmother Leyleira stood on his porch, her dark black hair flowing down her back over her green dress, the white streak in her hair prominent. Farrendel bowed his head. "Machasheni. What are you doing here?"

She had been residing at Lethorel, enjoying some rest away from the machinations of the court.

One of her eyebrows shot up. "My grandson is getting married. Of course I came. I am only sorry I was unable to arrive in time to greet you and your bride with the others. Now, may I come in?"

Farrendel nodded and stepped inside to allow her entry. She was his grandmother by blood just as much as she was Weylind's, Melantha's, and Jalissa's. Yet, Farrendel always felt like he could never fully claim her. As if he had no right to truly be a part of this family, even though the blood of the elven kings ran in his veins.

The door clicked shut behind his grandmother. She faced him, that eyebrow still raised. "Now, Farrendel. What is this I hear about you getting married for an alliance with the humans?"

He was not sure what information she was looking for. His grandmother's mind was still sharp as Farrendel's swords. She did not ask questions lightly, nor would she hesitate to parse every word he said until she examined each nuance of meaning, intentional or otherwise. "It was the condition the humans placed on the treaty. I was the most logical choice."

She stared at him, her gaze still piercing and unwavering. All but ordering him to keep talking.

"It was either marry her or risk more war and more killing." Farrendel gave a small shrug. "It seemed like the better option."

"The better option for you or the better option for your people?" Her tone was even, not giving away her own thoughts on the matter.

There was that eyebrow. How was Farrendel supposed to stay steady and not shift like a child caught stealing a treat from the kitchen? "Both. I do not wish to shed more blood. Nor do I wish to see elves and humans slaughter each other so needlessly."

"You would spare both elf and human lives?"

Why did she keep pushing this? "Yes."

A hint of a smile crossed his grandmother's face for a moment before she replaced it with her piercing gaze once more. "And your human bride? Is she as willingly marrying you for the sake of her people as you are for the sake of yours?"

Strangely, he did not have to think long about the answer. "Yes."

He braced himself for yet another lecture on not growing too attached to Princess Elspeth. Perhaps with another admonishment about the short lives of humans.

Machasheni stepped closer and rested a hand on his cheek. "Then I wish you every happiness with your bride, sasonsheni."

He rested his hands on her shoulders. Although he hesitated, his grandmother did not hold back from him.

Still, he let her words sink in. "You believe happiness is possible."

She patted his cheek, as if he was a small boy again. "Of course. Surely two people so willing to sacrifice themselves for the sake of their peoples will find a way to turn such deep love and loyalty toward each other."

Farrendel stumbled back. Had he heard that right? "First happiness, now love? You are not going to counsel me to avoid forming an attachment to the human?"

"Is that what your brother has been telling you? Pah." Machasheni Leyleira made the most undignified snorting sound he had ever heard from her. "Do not listen to him. You would think he would give better advice after the counsel I gave him when he married his Rheva. But he is young. He is not as wise as he thinks he is."

Only Machasheni Leyleira would talk so of the king. It was enough to ease the tension in Farrendel's shoulders. "What is your advice?"

"Choose her. Do not hold back." His grandmother patted his cheek again. "For years, you used to pick me and your sisters bouquets of flowers every day when we were at Lethorel. If you show this human princess that sweet boy I know is still in there somewhere, she will not be able to help loving you."

Farrendel grimaced. It had been a long, long time since he had been a child picking wildflowers for his grandmother. He was not sure he could remember how to be that innocently trusting.

"It will be difficult, especially as you are yet strangers." Her mouth tipped in a smile. "But I remember the days when stories were told of the great love that can exist between humans and elves."

"You speak of Daesyn and Inara." Farrendel could only blink at her. He had spent two days hearing nothing but lectures to not grow attached. That he could not hope for love or kindness or anything from this marriage but cold indifference at best.

More than that, she spoke not just of mere love. Daesyn was a human and Inara was an elf princess. Together, they formed an elishina, a heart bond, that was so strong, it lengthened Daesyn's life.

Surely his grandmother was not suggesting Farrendel and Princess Elspeth could form such a bond? They were strangers forced to marry to prevent a war between their peoples. Even in his best hopes, he did not dare believe an elishina was possible. He would be satisfied if they could even tolerate each other. "You have not even met her."

"No, but I peeked in to see if Jalissa needed aid. Jalissa and her maids have the preparations well in hand, so I left the matter in their capable hands." His grandmother bustled past him, headed toward the kitchen area of the room.

"You spied on them." He would have been more appalled, but this was his grandmother. It was not too unexpected coming from her.

She waved her hand, even as she set a satchel on the countertop, her back still to him. "I merely observed for the purpose of preparing the eshinelt. I do not believe she saw me."

As if that made spying so much better. But it did make him curious what his grandmother thought of Princess Elspeth. "And what was your impression of her, given your observations?"

Machasheni turned to face him, her eyebrow raised as if she knew he was doing the same type of questioning she usually wielded so skillfully. "She is currently attempting to make cheerful conversation with Jalissa and any of the maids who will stand still long enough to listen. Her mien is not that of someone forced or dreading this marriage. If anything, she is exuberant."

Exuberant was a good word for Princess Elspeth. Still, it was reassuring to hear she seemed to be coping all right with the situation. He would certainly not be so relaxed all alone in a foreign place.

"Her demeanor is surprising. She is the one giving up her home and people to come here with you, all with very little guarantee that she will not come to harm. That takes a great deal of courage." His grandmother gave him another smile, one of her cryptic smiles that said she knew something—or thought she knew something—that Farrendel did not. "Now. Come. I brought the ingredients for the eshinelt."

The eshinelt was the green paint used to draw ancient runes on each other during an elven wedding ceremony. But it was more than mere paint bought at one of the shops. It had to be prepared by the groom, the recipe usually passed down from parents to son.

"I know your father cannot be here. Weylind wished to do this, but I could tell he is against this marriage, for all that he is allowing it." Machasheni Leyleira began taking glass jars from the satchel on the countertop. "It would not do to have him help prepare the eshinelt."

As much as Farrendel wished Dacha could be here, he was glad Machasheni and not Weylind was in his place. It was good to have someone think he was making the right choice in this case. Perhaps she would weave some of her hope into the eshinelt, for hope was something he hardly dared to have recently.

He located a bowl, and Machasheni talked him through making the eshinelt. It involved crushing and mixing a variety of herbs, including mint, reminding Farrendel of the shampoo and conditioner he used. He had to choose from a selection of flowers and herbs Machasheni had brought for a scent that reminded him of Princess Elspeth. It was an intimate gesture, something that probably would not have been so awkward if he had known her longer than a day.

As he stirred it for what he assumed would be the last time, Machasheni gave a sharp nod. "Good. Now add in just a hint of your magic."

He dropped the spoon. "My magic?"

"Of course. That is the final ingredient."

"But my magic..." His magic would destroy the eshinelt. "Can you use your magic?"

His grandmother gave that snort again. "I am not the one getting married today. It must be you. Normally, this bowl would be carried to your bride as she prepares for the wedding, and she would add her own magic as well, but in your case, it will be your magic alone. Thankfully, yours is plenty strong for the both of you."

It was strong. That was the problem. It tended to incinerate anything it touched.

She huffed. "You used to do gentle sparks for Ryfon and Brina. I know you can control your magic enough for this."

It had been a long time since he had used his magic in such small quantities. Not since his father had died and he had become Laesornysh. Could he remember how to wield such small amounts when his magic pressed to be unleashed?

He would have to try. If he incinerated this eshinelt, hopefully Machasheni Leyleira had brought enough of the ingredients that they could make a second batch.

Farrendel called on his magic, letting it filter into bolts of blue lightning twining around his fingers.

Too much. Still too much. He reined it in, concentrating on letting just the hint of his magic dance on his fingers.

When it was nothing but sparks, he rubbed his fingers together over the bowl, as if adding in a pinch of herbs to a soup. The sparks fell into the eshinelt, and he quickly stirred it in. In his haste, he accidentally dropped more magic into it, and he quickly cut off his power. The eshinelt bubbled for a moment before falling still.

He had not destroyed it. That was a relief. But had he added too much magic? He glanced at his grandmother.

She smiled and nodded. "Well done. I do believe this will be a wedding that will be talked about for centuries to come."

Farrendel winced. What did she mean by that? He did not dare ask.

Most likely, this would be a scandal only rivaled by the illegitimacy of his birth.

SEVEN

F arrendel stood before his mirror and shakily tugged on the hem of his tunic, attempting to adjust it to hide his scars.

It did little good. Without a shirt underneath the tunic, he could not cover them all. The tunic's half sleeves stopped above his elbows while a large V of his chest remained exposed. At least the worst of the scars across his shoulders and upper arms were covered. But the scars down his arms, especially at his wrists, were plainly visible for all to see.

What would Princess Elspeth think, seeing how scarred and battered he was? For she would see. As close as they would stand during the ceremony, she could not help but notice.

He already knew what the elven court—those same court nobles that Weylind had to threaten to make them attend—would think. They would scorn. Judge. Curl their mouths in disgust.

He would have to stand before them like this and endure it.

And Weylind thought that marrying a human was the hardest part of today. No, marrying Princess Elspeth was the least of his concerns for that evening.

The brush of Weylind's footsteps on the stairs gave warning even before Weylind knocked on the frame of Farrendel's door. When Farrendel did not tell him to go away, the door opened, and Weylind stepped inside. "Everyone is assembled. Your bride is nearly ready."

Farrendel gave another tug on the tunic, trying to get it to stay in place over a long scar that cut across his chest down to his stomach. "I am ready."

"Here." Weylind held out a pair of archer's vambraces. They were more decorative than those used in battle, with oiled brown leather and silver engraving. "These will help."

It was not traditional, but Princess Elspeth would not know the difference. Nor would anyone in attendance question why Farrendel was covering most of his arms.

He pulled them on. The vambraces covered his wrists and his forearms nearly up to his elbows. Between the half sleeve of the tunic and the vambrace, only a small portion of his arm around his elbow was visible, and that portion had fewer scars than his wrists and shoulders. He started to tie the laces. "Linshi."

Weylind reached out and tightened the laces for him. "Are you still sure you wish to do this?"

Farrendel gritted his teeth and met Weylind's gaze. "Yes."

Weylind sighed as he tied the vambrace laces. "Very well. Machasheni already gave me a lecture. I have no wish to incur another one by arguing."

How Farrendel had managed to get their grandmother on his side in this, he was not sure. But he was thankful. She was a force to be reckoned with. "She seemed pleased."

"That is what worries me," Weylind muttered. He shook his head, then grasped Farrendel's upper arms, meeting his gaze. "Dacha would have been proud today."

Those words ached so fiercely, Farrendel could not breathe for a moment, much less move. It was harder and harder to remember the laughter and the warmth his father had. Every time he thought of Dacha, his mind yanked him to those last moments. The terrible sound of the arrow plunging into Dacha's back. The blood. The gasping breaths. The way his father had held him, shielding him, even as he was dying.

If Farrendel ached, missing his father today, he only had himself to blame. If he had been strong enough to protect his father during that rescue or if he had avoided being captured in the first place, Dacha would still be alive.

Instead, he had died. Because of Farrendel.

That reminder hardened Farrendel's jaw. His grandmother's visit earlier made him think hope was possible, but he could not allow himself to believe that. He could not allow himself to dream about happiness for he knew how easily it could get snatched away.

He stepped out of his brother's grasp. "Let's get this done."

Not the most romantic or hopeful statement, but at that moment, all Farrendel wanted was for this wedding to be over.

FARRENDEL STOOD at the front of the hall, trying to ignore the horde of courtiers seated in the large room. The hall was grown at the very heart of Ellonahshinel with massive branches arching overhead to form the ceiling while gold glittered as it gilded the small twigs and patterns in the bark. Rows of windows overlooked Estyra and the surrounding forest, letting the beams of the setting sun fall in patterns on the floor and far wall.

Avoiding the gaze of most of those in the crowd, Farrendel focused on the far back of the room. There, a few of his friends among the army had been allowed to slip into the back once the front rows had been filled with the courtiers. It was the unfair part about being an elf prince. Even though the courtiers did not care for him nor he for them, they still showed up for his wedding and still insisted on being shown deference while the people Farrendel actually wanted at his wedding were relegated to the far back.

But even with the snub dealt them, his friends had come anyway. Illyna, Fingol, and many others crammed into the final row despite the disgusted looks they were getting for the missing hand, damaged foot that caused a limp, burn scars, and other wounds they had suffered during the wars with the trolls and humans.

They understood, probably more than anyone, why he was willing to do this.

The sound of distant singing, high and ethereal, wafted on the slight breeze. His sisters, singing the traditional song for Princess Elspeth as she made her way to the hall.

Farrendel's chest tightened, even as he hardened his face against displaying any hint of his emotion. He should not be this nervous, considering he had already married her once. He just had to survive this ceremony and then…

And then what? He could not even picture what tomorrow would look like. Change rarely brought good things.

The double doors at the far end of the room opened, and Princess Elspeth stepped inside, her hair a flaming red beacon against her white dress.

Even with all his struggle for self-control, he caught his breath. Somehow, the seamstresses had turned the white, poofy dress into something that flowed down the princess's form into a graceful train behind her.

What was wrong with him? Somehow, his brain had gone foggy, and he struggled to keep his breathing even and steady.

Princess Elspeth halted at the front and turned to face him, though her gaze latched onto a spot lower than his face.

His scars. He resisted the urge to tug on the tunic to better hide them.

Trembling slightly, she dragged her gaze to meet his, her eyes wide. Was she as nervous as he was?

Most of the ceremony passed in a blur. All too soon, Weylind picked up the shallow bowl containing the eshinelt and held it out to Princess Elspeth. Her face paling slightly, she took it and faced Farrendel with her shoulders squared, her stance stiff.

Farrendel dipped his finger into the eshinelt. It was cold to his touch and would probably feel even colder against her skin. He mentally apologized as he touched her forehead as gently as possible and traced an ancient elvish rune with the green eshinelt on her skin. "May our minds sharpen each other and may we always provide each other wise counsel."

She held still beneath his touch, her gaze focusing on the bowl she held rather than his face.

He dipped his finger in again and formed the next rune on her right cheek, trying to ignore the adorable sprinkle of freckles across her nose. "May our speech be filled with kindness, gentleness, and understanding."

As he dipped his finger into the eshinelt for a third time, she visibly braced herself, the slight tremor in her fingers sending ripples across the eshinelt's surface.

As gently as he could, he traced the final rune on her upper chest above her heart well above the neckline of her dress, feeling her shiver beneath his touch. "May our hearts be bound as one for all our days together."

She flinched, sucking in a breath. Her gaze flicked to him, then back to the bowl.

What was wrong? He searched her face. He had kept his magic well buried. He could feel only a tingle of it in the eshinelt. Not enough to hurt, surely.

Whatever had just happened, she regained her composure quickly and held the bowl out to him. He took it and found himself bracing much as she had. This was a ceremony meant for those well and truly in love, not strangers who found it highly awkward.

She dipped her finger into the eshinelt, bit her lip, and tentatively reached out. It took all his self-control to stand still and not bolt from the hall.

Her touch was soft, the eshinelt cold against his forehead. He could not tell if she had drawn the rune correctly, though she did swipe her finger in some kind of pattern.

She spoke the blessing in halting elvish, her tone

monotone as she recited memorized words. Her pronunciation was terrible, made even worse by an Escarlish accent so thick it would take a sword to cut through it.

Not that he could blame her. He, at least, could speak and read the words he had memorized for the Escarlish wedding. She did not know elvish and thus had memorized patterns of sounds that had no real meaning for her. The fact that even a few of the words were understandable was amazing.

She repeated the process with the rune on his cheek, her pronunciation a mess.

She dipped her finger into the eshinelt a third time and touched his chest over his heart, feather-light and gentle.

His heart pounded, and it was all he could do to stand there. A part of him wanted to shove her hand away, memories of torture and pain all too close to the surface.

And yet tingles spread down his spine, and another part of him did not want her to stop. His mouth went dry.

Then her finger paused partway through the rune. She swayed slightly closer, her gaze focused.

She was definitely inspecting his scars this time. It was a cold dousing, and he stiffened with it. He was scarred. Flawed. Someone who ended up destroying everything around him.

Yes, Weylind was right. It was best not to grow too attached. Not for his sake, but for hers.

With a slight shake of her head, she quickly finished the rune and rushed through the final blessing.

As she said the last word, magic, like the shock of one of his lightning bolts of power, surged from the spot where her finger rested to deep inside Farrendel's chest. The intensity of it was enough to make him flinch.

What was that? Was that his magic, accidentally too strong in the eshinelt? Yet, if that were the case, then why had he not felt it when saying the blessings for her?

This surge of magic was tied to the final blessing, and she had flinched as well when he had said that same blessing for her. Was this normal? Perhaps this was the expected magical binding of hearts that was supposed to take place due to those blessings. The eshinelt was prepared to encourage such a binding.

He could not count on his grandmother to have warned him about something like this, but surely Weylind might have mentioned it if such a powerful surge of magic binding them together was to be expected.

Unless it was not expected between a human and an elf. Maybe Weylind had failed to mention it since he believed it would not occur for this wedding.

Farrendel was not sure whom he would ask for answers. His grandmother, maybe. If she could be persuaded to answer his questions in a straightforward manner instead of with more questions of her own. Perhaps Weylind, though Farrendel was not sure he wanted his brother to know that some kind of magical bonding had taken place.

Even though Princess Elspeth was a human, the elven blessings had worked as they were intended. For all that Weylind did not like it, Farrendel and Princess Elspeth were well and truly, twice-over married and magically bound.

And that meant Machasheni Leyleira, not Weylind, had been right all along.

He glanced toward his grandmother where she sat tall and regal in the front row. When he met her gaze, her mouth curled in a smile, her eyes twinkling, and she tipped her head in a slight nod.

Machasheni approved. Somehow, even though she had yet to speak to Princess Elspeth directly, the little that Machasheni had observed had been enough to earn her approval, a thing not easily granted.

It kindled that warmth that almost felt like hope in Farrendel's chest. Maybe this marriage could work and—dare he even think it?—be a happy one.

FROM HIS SEAT behind the table set up on the dais, Farrendel eyed the whirling dancers filling the hall below. Perhaps he should ask his wife to dance. It would certainly be expected of the newly married couple, and, beside him, Princess Elspeth was leaning forward, her eyes focused on the dancing as if she would be interested in trying it.

But Farrendel normally avoided the dancing at court events...or any event in general. He had even avoided dancing at Fingol's wedding last year, and that had been a small gathering, especially compared to this.

The thought of so many eyes watching him as he whirled through the steps, unable to safely keep his back to a wall as he was surrounded by a crush of other people...it sent shudders down his back.

Perhaps it was time to make a swift exit and end this torture of an evening. He would much rather be alone with Princess Elspeth—as awkward as it was—than stay here.

When he stood and held out his arm to her, she jumped to her feet as if she had been just as eager to leave as he was. She reached for his elbow, halted, then rested her hand on his forearm in the elven style.

He kept his head down as they skirted the edge of the hall and exited, having no wish to meet anyone's eye and see their knowing smirk. Or, worse, be drawn into a conversation. He had already used up all his words for one evening.

Outside, the cool evening air brushed away the stifling press of people, clearing his head for the first time in hours. As he drew in a deep breath, Princess Elspeth's shoulders were rising and falling beside him, as if she too were gulping in the fresh air after being stuck with too many people.

When she seemed ready, Farrendel led her up staircases and across branches toward his rooms far from the bustle at the center of Ellonahshinel. Darkness blanketed the treetops, the branches lit only by a few magical globes of light strategically placed along the pathways.

The farther they walked, the more Princess Elspeth leaned against him, her fingers tightening on his arm until her grip was almost painful. What was wrong?

At the last branch leading to his rooms, Princess Elspeth halted, her face draining of color until it nearly matched the white dress she wore. She backed away, her grip leaving his arm as she wrapped both arms around her stomach.

He turned to her, studying her face. She was petrified of something. Was she afraid of what would happen once they were alone in his rooms? He swallowed, not sure of a proper way of going about reassuring her.

This was an arranged marriage. He was not sure what she was expecting, but he had every intention of bolting for his room. Alone. By himself. Trust, after all, took time.

Her shoulders rose and fell in quick, shuddering breaths, and her voice came out an octave higher than normal. "I take it there aren't any clumsy elves? Not that I'm terribly clumsy for a human, but humans do tend to have accidents happen to us, and that branch is awfully small to walk across. My balance isn't quite like yours."

His muscles relaxed. Ah. That was her fear.

Having grown up walking the treetops, it had not occurred to him what navigating Ellonahshinel would be like for someone who had spent her life on the ground. From what he had seen of the human outpost, humans did not appear to like heights.

He could handle this concern. Perhaps not easily, but better than having to find the words to address...other things.

Though, what should he do now? He could carry her across. He had been reluctant to carry her to the bed in the train, but that had been when she had been asleep and unable to tell him if she did not wish it.

Farrendel closed the distance between them and bent to pick her up, opening his mouth as he tried to find the words to ask if she would allow this.

"No, wait!" She backed up yet again, an edge of panic to her voice.

He froze. He had messed up and frightened her. Not his intention. What should he do or say to reassure her?

"Sorry. I just...I can do this. I have to do this. I'm going to be living here, and I have to get used to walking across these branches." She inched forward, her back stiff, her fingers clenched. Her chin lifted as she faced him, though he was not sure whether she was challenging him or the branch ahead of them.

Did she want help or not want help? She did not wish

to be picked up, yet she also seemed like she wanted something from him.

Perhaps if he walked slower this time. Let her ease across the branch at her own pace instead of his.

He eased upright and held out his arm again. This time, she latched onto his upper arm with both hands as if afraid the darkness below would try to tear her away and drag her down.

He probably should say something soothing or reassuring. But his tongue was stuck to the roof of his mouth, and his brain could not seem to process words.

Instead, he inched across the branch, letting her steady herself between each step before he took the next one.

She took a step, then tottered. Her gaze darted to the drop below, her face somehow paling even further. Her breathing turned into gasps, and she flailed for him as if she were a vine trying to latch on to a tree's bark to begin twining upward.

It was instinct to put his arms around her, steadying her. She did not flinch away but held him tighter, her knuckles brushing his skin as she gripped his tunic.

She tore her gaze away from the drop to stare instead at his chest, the stiffness in her muscles relaxing a fraction. She swayed closer still.

Could she hear the way his heart was beating faster? His mouth had gone dry as sunbaked earth, his head as light and dizzy as if he were suffering vertigo from the heights they walked.

He could not be…this was not…was it possible he was attracted to her?

She looked up and met his gaze, her eyes more green than blue in the faint light of the nearest globe. And he found himself struggling to breathe, wanting to stay like that with her warm in the circle of his arms.

What magic was this that muddled his thinking so? He forced himself to ease back, putting distance between them. He knew little of her. She knew little of him. Apparently, he was attracted to her, but he did not know if she was attracted to him or if she simply was grateful he had not let her fall.

All of Machasheni's talk of love and stories and elishinas had gone to his head. That was it.

He finally dragged up the words he should have said at the beginning of the branch. "Relax."

She eased back, her grip on his tunic releasing as she switched her fingers back to his arm.

He held her elbows to continue steadying her while holding her at a distance. "If you are tense, you will fall."

She drew in a deep breath and nodded, that set to her chin returning.

Good. Whatever that strangeness from a moment ago, he could put it behind him and ignore it.

He eased backwards along the branch. He did not need to see where he was going, this path familiar, his senses telling him exactly where the branch and his rooms lay.

She took a few more steps, then glanced down, her balance wobbling again.

Farrendel tightened his grip, steadying her. "Do not look down."

Her gaze latched onto his, her eyes wide. Yet something in her gaze seemed trusting.

That trust stabbed into his chest. How much trust did it take for her to follow him across this branch? He was at no risk of falling, but she apparently was. She was trusting him with her life at the moment, and he was so unworthy of it.

Yet, somehow, she was giving it anyway. She held his gaze as he led the rest of the way across the branch until finally his heel bumped into the step of the porch surrounding the main room. As he stepped up, she followed, gaze unwavering from his. "We are here."

She blinked, then looked around at her surroundings.

He was not sure what she would think of his home. This main room was small compared to the rooms his siblings occupied, though still constructed of arching branches grown in intricate designs as they formed the walls, ceiling, and floor.

As Farrendel led the way inside, he spoke the word to activate the globes lighting the space, setting the lighting level to a warm yellow glow rather than the whiter daylight brightness.

Princess Elspeth stepped inside, her gaze sweeping everything. A hint of a smile returned, so the space must not have appalled her too greatly. Though, a small furrow appeared on her forehead, the smile dimming, as she took in the cupboards of the kitchen. Was this too humble and modest compared to her own kitchen in her suite of rooms in the human palace?

After long moments surveying the room, she turned to him, something hesitant and almost wary tightening her expression.

That panicky feeling clawed its way back into his chest. There was that topic they still had to address. Sleeping arrangements.

Even without a shirt beneath his wedding tunic, his skin burned too hot, and he turned from her, unable to meet her gaze.

Best just to pretend this was not a topic they had to discuss and act like it had already been decided. It would take far fewer words that way.

He strode across the room and pointed at the door to what had once been a guest room. "This is your room."

The skin on his back prickled beneath the weight of her gaze, the spot between his shoulder blades itching as if expecting a stabbing knife at any moment. The walls of the room closed in, his lungs tight.

Get away. He had to get away. Now.

He flung open the door to his room, managing to force out a quick, "This one is mine," before he dove through the doorway. At the last moment, he remembered to shut the door quietly instead of slamming it between them.

Farrendel leaned against the door to the stairs to his room, his back braced against it as if to keep himself upright. He drew in several deep breaths, calming his racing heartbeat and clearing his head.

What an undignified exit. She was not a troll warrior waiting to kill him. She was his wife. What would she think of him now? Why could he not talk like a normal elf?

He should have said goodnight. It was one word. That was all. How hard would it have been?

He should go back in there and tell her goodnight. Yes. That was what he would do. With a deep breath, he reached for the door handle.

But before he could open the door, he heard the creak of the other door, then Princess Elspeth's footsteps as she climbed the stairs to her room.

He could call out to her now, but as it was fully dark, it would probably frighten her. The last thing he needed to do was startle her into slipping and falling to her death.

The door of her treehouse room slammed shut behind her.

Farrendel winced and sank slowly to the floor with his back to the door. That…did not go well. At all.

Perhaps this marriage could work. Maybe they would find love. If he wanted to think about impossible dreams, then they might even form a heart bond and build a lasting peace between their two kingdoms.

But that would only happen if he could manage to actually talk to his wife.

Farrendel leaned his head against the door behind him and whispered, "Goodnight, Princess Elspeth…Essie."

His only answer was the gentle nighttime breeze wafting against his skin and stirring the strands of his hair across his shoulders.

Tomorrow. He would do better tomorrow.

EIGHT

F arrendel pushed himself harder, faster, as he raced along the two-inch-wide branch. If he ran fast enough, maybe he could outrun the swirling thoughts tangling his brain and tightening his chest. He had barely slept, not with the human princess sleeping in the room on the next branch.

Princess Elspeth. His *wife*.

He was married. He had a wife.

Do not think. Do not feel. He launched himself into a front somersault, adding a twist to the somersault so that he faced back the way he had come.

What in Tarenhiel was he supposed to do now? Was he doing enough? He had left a plate with breakfast on the counter for Princess Elspeth when she woke. Should he have done more?

No, not Princess Elspeth. Essie. That was what she said to call her, strange as a shortened name seemed.

Should he have waited in the main room for her? He had tried waiting for a few minutes, but he had started shaking, his chest and stomach so tight he had barely managed a few bites of his own breakfast.

Do not think. Do not feel. He pushed his muscles until they loosened, then burned with exertion. He spun and leapt and flipped until sweat dripped down his face and trickled between his shoulder blades. Until, finally, the racing thoughts steadied enough to make him feel he could face the day.

He pushed himself for one last sprint, then flipped over the railing, landing in a crouch.

Essie was there. Right there. Just sitting on the floor of the porch, staring at him.

He should run.

He had to stay.

No matter. He could not force himself to move. She was there and she was staring and his head was back to dizzy, his stomach churning.

"I, um..." Her gaze flicked from the floor to him and back several times, as if she was not sure where to look. "I didn't know where you were and then...you have..." Her voice lowered. "A lot of scars."

Of course. His scars. She had stared during the wedding—everyone always stared—and the scars were making her uncomfortable now too. He swung his gaze to the floor, his skin crawling. His shirt. He needed his shirt. "I will cover them."

As his fingers closed over the fabric, she grabbed his shirt as well. "Sorry, that didn't come out like I meant it to. Your scars don't bother me."

She was just saying that, hiding her disgust.

His chest squeezed, one breath away from breaking into ragged gasps. His skin had gone past crawling to the point of something almost like pain.

He needed his shirt. He had to cover the scars. The disgust. The prying eyes scouring him.

But when he gave a light tug on the fabric, her grip didn't budge.

He could run. He could let go of his shirt, dive through the window, and hide until she went away.

Yet he could not seem to talk his hand into letting go. He was paralyzed with the panic.

Just as he talked himself into running, Essie released his shirt, her voice quiet as she spoke. "Where I come from, a scarred warrior is honored. It means he has faced battle and death and survived. Scars are something about which the men boast and the women admire."

Surely she could not mean that.

She was a human. And humans had a different culture and way of looking at things. He hardly dared let himself hope. He had expected her to be disgusted at his scars. Hoped that she might eventually tolerate them.

But admire the scars? Was such a thing even possible?

He gathered the last shreds of courage he had left and lifted his gaze from his shirt to her face.

Nothing in her expression—from her kind green eyes to her soft smile—indicated that she was anything other than sincere.

Not that he was a good judge of people or their expressions. She could be hiding all manner of thoughts, and he would never be able to guess them.

No, he could not keep thinking like this. Last night, he had told himself that he would try. If he was going to make something out of this marriage, then he could not doubt her at every turn. Instead, he would have to do something that went against all his instincts and trust her.

She had demonstrated a lot of trust in him in the past

couple of days. He had to give her his best attempt at trust in return.

He held her gaze, struggling to think of something, anything, to say.

She leaned forward and slowly reached out.

What was she...surely she was not...Farrendel still could not bring himself to move.

Then her fingers gently, lightly, brushed his cheek over the place where his childhood scar marred his skin.

She was touching him. She was touching his face. It was as if a bolt of his magic went off in his brain and fried every logical thought in his head.

Her smile tipped wider, though something about her remained soft. "I don't know how scars are viewed by your people, but the only thing I mind about your scars is the suffering you must have gone through to get them. But you survived, and for that, I admire you, scars and all."

Her words soothed the tension from his spine and released him from the paralysis that had gripped him since he had found her there, watching him.

He forced his fingers to unclench from his shirt, then he sat on the floor, facing her. He still could not dredge up any words, but hopefully if he sat there long enough, she would start talking, saving him from having to do so.

She studied him, her eyebrows furrowed. He could almost see her mind whirling, the thoughts flicking through her eyes.

After several long, silent minutes, she smiled once again. "It's a good thing you married me, then."

What had she been thinking about for her to come to that conclusion?

If anything, her smile quirked into something teasing

as she gestured at him. "Since I find all of this rather attractive."

Farrendel gaped. What...had she just...surely she... His brain felt all magic-fried once again. His ears were on fire, and he had to duck his head again, hoping his hair covered his face and ears.

She sighed, and when she spoke, her tone had changed to serious. "We need to talk."

Farrendel peeked at her but did not move. What did she want from him? It had almost seemed like she was flirting with him. Maybe, he was not sure. Now she was all serious.

He could read a battlefield and outmaneuver his opponents, but simply talking with this human bride of his was the most bewildering situation he had ever been in.

Silence had worked so far. Perhaps it would keep working.

Essie dropped her gaze to her lap, and after a moment, she did indeed start talking again, this time at a rapid, breathless pace. "I need to know what you expect from this marriage and from me. I don't want to embarrass you or make you regret marrying me any more than you already do, but I don't know elven culture well. If I'm doing something wrong or there's something I should know, then please tell me. I won't always know the right questions to ask."

What *he* expected? He had no expectations. If he could process his thoughts quickly enough, then he would ask all those same questions back to her.

But before he could think of anything to say, she drew in a deep breath and kept talking with barely a pause. "I know I'm probably not the wife you expected to marry someday, and you didn't have any more time to prepare for this wedding than I did. I know love probably isn't an option, but I'm willing to put an effort into at least making this a really good friendship."

Wait, love? Friendship? She...she actually wanted that?

"I'm willing to be the person you can trust and confide in and smile with you. But I need to know you're going to put an effort in too and aren't just going to go about your day ignoring me. It's hard to know what you're thinking when you don't even talk to me and I don't know if you find me annoying or you don't understand half of what I'm saying. I just..." She blew out a breath, her hands gesturing, then flopping into her lap, as she fell silent.

He should not hope. He should not let his heart beat harder, painful, at the thought of smiles and friendship and trust.

It was impossible. He could not risk giving away the shreds that he had left of his heart.

Then again, what did he really have left to lose? If this fell apart, he would simply trade the misery of a war with Escarland for misery of a marriage to a wife who hated him. At least in that case, he would be the only one paying the price.

Besides, his family would still be there. They would protect him as needed. He would not be alone.

But if this actually turned into the friendship she was offering? If this spark he felt in his chest when he looked at her formed into something real?

Essie remained sitting there, watching him with a slight smile playing on her mouth. The morning sunlight glinted in her fiery hair, and he had the sudden urge to run his fingers through its strands.

Words. He had to say something. Anything.

He could not think while looking at her. He dropped his gaze, drew in a deep breath, and forced himself to speak. "I do not want to say anything to offend you."

Essie's smile bloomed into a grin, her green eyes sparkling. "You won't offend me. I've been saying the first things that come to my mind this whole time, and I haven't offended you. Or I don't think I have. Would you even tell me if I offended you? Will you at least tell me if something I say is considered horribly offensive to elven culture so I know not to say it in the future?"

Of course he would tell her, if he could find the words in the moment. He managed a nod, then forced himself to speak yet again. She had been pouring her heart out to him, and she deserved that he do the same. "I like when you talk."

She opened her mouth, then snapped it shut, meeting his gaze with something almost like a dare.

Great, she wanted him to talk again?

He said the first thing that came to him. "When I wait, you keep on talking. It is humorous."

As soon as the words popped from his mouth, he could have gladly cut out his own tongue. Seriously. She might think he was insulting her.

Yet, instead of yelling at him, she gave a laugh, her grin never wavering. "Thanks for telling me. Now I can laugh inwardly along with you. I'm glad you find me entertaining."

So maybe that bit of honesty had not gone astray. Would she react just as well if he continued to be honest? He stared at his hands as he admitted, "There has not been much that is humorous in my life."

Her hand came into his line of sight before resting on his knee.

She was touching him. Again. His brain swirled, stuck. Her hand was on his knee. *On his knee.*

It was all he could do to tear his gaze away to look up at her.

Her smile remained in place, though her eyes held a depth that he could not read. "Then I am especially glad you find me humorous. I will endeavor to be plenty ridiculous. I may even see you smile some day."

Why would she want to see his smile? Surely only someone who cared for him would want to see him happy. But she barely knew him. She could not possibly care.

He could not face her. He could not let her see his hope.

She withdrew her hand from his knee, and his skin felt strangely cold even through the layer of his trousers. A shiver prickled the bare skin of his back and chest, reminding him that he still lacked his shirt.

"So what do we do now?" Her tone went back to light and cheery. "I would love to see more of the palace and the city."

He tried to imagine walking around Ellonahshinel or Estyra with her next to him. The stares. The questions. Having to explain over and over. Talking to people.

He could not. It was too much, too soon. Whatever they did today, he needed to stay here. Away from other people. "It would be...unusual for us to venture anywhere this week, but especially today."

Ugh, were his ears burning again? Why did he have to use that excuse to stay in today?

Essie did not seem to share his embarrassment. She

just nodded, still smiling. "I see. It would be unusual for a couple in my kingdom to go out and about the day after the wedding too. Though, considering our circumstances, it might not be totally unexpected."

Oh, good. She understood.

"Why don't we stay here and talk today?" Elspeth waved over her shoulder toward the main room. "Well, maybe not here specifically. Maybe down there where we can sit on those comfy cushions. At least I think they are comfy. I haven't tested them out yet. Is that all right with you? I don't even know how old you are or your favorite color or anything like that. And you can ask me questions. As you've probably learned, I would be happy to answer anything you want to ask. Then tomorrow maybe we can see some of Estyra. Touring the palace can wait."

Talking. Surely he could manage talking. It was not the relaxing hiding that he had in mind, but as long as she provided most of the chatter, he could handle it. Maybe.

Besides, spending time with her did not sound all that bad. Nor did visiting Estyra, after he had a day to hide away from people here.

It might even be fun, to see more of that wide-eyed wonder on her face, like their brief walk from the train to Ellonahshinel.

Farrendel forced a nod. "There is a back way to leave to visit Estyra. I would...like to avoid my family. They are protective."

The last thing he wanted to do was face Weylind's scowl right now. Weylind meant well, but Farrendel had enough to sort out without enduring that glower.

She let out such a loud sigh, even he could read her relief. "That sounds fine by me. It would be nice to be more sure of myself here before facing your protective siblings. I am even kind of glad my siblings are a kingdom away. They are just as protective of me and suspicious of you as your family is of me."

Her wry admission stirred something in his chest. As if a smile tugging at his face was not such a remote possibility as he had thought. "I know."

Her mouth twisted in an exaggerated wince. "Yes, sorry about my brothers cornering you at the wedding. They probably would have been threatening even if I'd married a human, but they were more so because you're an elf. Sorry."

He was not sorry. He had found their threat almost humorous rather than offensive. "They value you."

"As your family does you." She stated it firmly, as if she had no doubt that her words were true.

He could not hold her gaze. Yes, his family valued him. More than they should, considering his illegitimate birth.

Essie hopped to her feet. "I'll meet you in the main room, if you want to wash up after your morning routine."

Farrendel pushed to his feet, even as she started to turn away. Something twisted in his chest. He was supposed to call her Essie, but he could not bring himself to say anything but her full name out loud. It seemed disrespectful otherwise. "Elspeth?"

She froze, then turned back toward him, her eyes searching his face. "Yes?"

Why had he called her back? What was so important that he had to tell her?

His heart hurt inside his chest, aching and full. She had been so trusting, so vulnerable with him so far that morning. He should trust her in return, even if he could not meet her gaze as he did. "I do not regret marrying you."

A warm smile spread across her face, her eyes lighting. "I don't regret marrying you either."

She spun and hurried back the way she had come, disappearing around the corner of his room.

As soon as she was out of sight, Farrendel sagged against the wall, his hands trembling. What just happened? Had that gone well? Or terribly? He was not entirely sure which one it was.

Even worse, he would have to face her all over again in a few minutes.

CHAPTER
NINE

Farrendel let the hot water pound into his head
and back. He was taking far too long. Essie was
waiting, and he was delaying as long as he
could.

He could do this. He had to do this. They were just
going to talk. Not that scary, right?

Wrong. Terrifying. Utterly terrifying. If he did not get
a hold of his stomach, he was going to lose the little
breakfast he had managed to eat.

When he finally admitted he could not make her wait
any longer, he dressed and walked down the stairs, his
heart pounding harder with each step. Stomach churning,
he pulled open the door to the main room.

Inside, Essie sat on one of the cushions, bouncing a
little. Her gaze snapped up to him, and she stilled, a smile
on her face.

Do not panic. Do *not* panic.

He forced himself to cross the room and sit on one of
the cushions a few feet away from her, his back safely to

the wall. It took all his self-control to keep his churning stomach in place, and he hid his shaking hands by clenching them against his knees.

Essie would have to start the conversation. Farrendel was not about to.

"Um, well, do you have any questions? Because I have a lot of questions." Essie's gaze flicked over his face. "Don't let me ask all the questions, all right?"

She paused, as if expecting something from him.

He forced himself to nod.

That seemed to satisfy her. "My favorite color is dark green. Mostly because of this." She picked up her long braid and waggled it. "Green always looks good with my hair. Blue too. But the other colors can be iffy, depending on the shade. It makes it difficult when picking out fabric for dresses. But green is my dependable color. What's your favorite color?"

Why did she want to know his favorite color? Of everything they had to talk about, why was she starting with something so trivial?

Yet trivial was easier to handle than something personal and vulnerable. It took a moment, but he managed to get the single word out. "Blue."

Essie leaned against the wall behind her, all of her muscles relaxed. As if this was not difficult for her in the least. She faced him with that easy smile. "How old are you?"

"One hundred and five." Farrendel was not sure what she would make of that information.

She grinned, giving a smothered sound that might have been a laugh before shaking her head. "That makes you something like nineteen or so years old in human years."

By the tone of her voice, she found that terribly young. How old was she? Farrendel had not thought her much older than him, but what if Weylind was right and she was?

Farrendel ducked his head, unable to meet her gaze. "One hundred and five is scandalously young for an elf to marry."

"Nineteen is somewhat young for humans as well. Not scandalously young, though." Essie's voice still held a trace of a laugh. "I'm twenty. Does that make me a hundred and ten or twenty or something like that to you elves?"

Oh, good. She was still younger than two hundred and within what would be considered an acceptable age gap for married couples. Weylind's fear had been unfounded, even if she was indeed older than Farrendel.

Perhaps it was the relief, but he found the tension in his muscles easing. "Still young. Elves consider it best to wait to marry until full maturity at one hundred fifty to two hundred."

"I guess when you have the luxury of nearly a thousand years of life, waiting doesn't hurt." When she spoke, Essie gestured with her hands, every word and movement confident and easy, as if she was not worried in the least what he might think of her or what she said. "We humans tend to marry young. Not everyone does. Avie didn't get married until he was twenty-three, and both Julien and Edmund will probably be at least that if not older before either of them even thinks about marriage. When you only live eighty to ninety years or so, every year counts."

Her smile faded, and she glanced away from him for the first time.

He was not good with people, but Essie's open emotions were easier to read than most. Nor did it take an expert to see that she was missing her family.

What could he do? What could he offer her?

He was the one who had taken her away from that family. Did she blame him?

Before he could come up with anything to say, she smiled again and faced him, leaning forward. "Do you have a question you would like to ask? I've asked two."

With her inviting tone and expression, some of the churning in his stomach faded. This talking with her was not so bad, after all.

And there was one question he had wanted to ask. "Why do your people shorten your names?"

"Like a nickname?" Essie's eyebrows lifted.

So that was what they were called.

She shrugged. "Usually because it is shorter and quicker to say than a person's full name. But nicknames are also endearments. Usually only close family and friends will use a nickname."

Now he understood. It was not a mere shortening of her name. But a nickname was a special name for family and friends to use. And when Essie gave him the use of her nickname, she was telling him that he now had a family relationship with her.

She had also given Weylind and Farrendel's siblings the use of her nickname. She had been adopting all of his family as her family, and he had not even realized it.

The others would never use that nickname. They would not understand, as he had not. Nor did he really want to explain, not if it meant that the name Essie could be something special that he, and he alone here in Taren-hiel, would call her.

"Don't you use nicknames?"

Oh, she had asked another question. He quickly shook his head. "No. Our names have meaning. To shorten them would take away the meaning."

She nodded, her forehead furrowing. "What does Farrendel mean?"

He should have expected this question. Bracing himself, he touched a strand of his silver-blond hair. "Fair One."

Well, it was more like *The One with the Fair Hair* but *Fair One* was close enough.

With a twist to her mouth, she tugged her braid over her shoulder. "I would've been named after my hair color too. It's rather bright."

Was that a scowl? And a note of deprecation in her voice? Why would she sound like that when talking about her hair? "It is pretty."

He snapped his mouth shut, the tips of his ears burning. This was why he did not talk. He just ended up embarrassing himself whenever he did.

Instead of shifting in embarrassment, a brilliant smile flashed onto her face, lighting her eyes into a brighter green. "I'm glad you think so. Back in Escarland, a lot of people dismiss it as a vulgar color. And they expect me to get angry easily because, of course, I must have a terrible temper."

"Why would they think you have a temper?" He had to be missing something. What did red hair have to do with a temper?

"For some reason, people associate red hair with getting angry easily. As if red hair has anything to do with it." For the first time, there was a note of heat in her voice, before it disappeared in another smile. "Ask me another question."

Perhaps it was the reference to her culture, but his next question came out without too much thought. "What is it like in your kingdom?"

It turned out to be the right question. When Essie started talking about Escarland, she just kept on going, describing the city of Aldon and Winstead Palace before moving on to talk about her family and friends.

Her whole face lit up, her voice warm and filled with laughter and memories. Farrendel could not help but stare at her, watching the fascinating play of easy smiles and laughter in her expression.

Joy. A deep, inner joy. That was what he was seeing in her. It was fascinating. And beautiful. And bewildering. He could listen to her all day.

As she paused for a breath, a loud gurgling sound came from the direction of her stomach. She shifted, an arm wrapping over her middle.

Farrendel glanced to the window, then shoved to his feet. He had been so wrapped up in listening to her that he had not noticed the time. She must think him neglectful, letting her talk through lunchtime.

She started to push to her feet, but Farrendel quickly gestured for her to stay where she was. When she hesitated, he shook his head. "Stay."

He would rather she kept talking than have her help preparing food for lunch.

As he opened the cold cupboard, she relaxed back onto the cushion and resumed the story she had been telling about her brothers Prince Julien and Prince Edmund stealing King Averett's crown. It was a rather humorous story and shed a different light on her brothers than the glowering, angry men he had met at the wedding.

The options stocked in the cold cupboard were simple. Bread. Some cooked venison that could be eaten cold. Leftover *frishk*, a vegetable and venison mash that also could be eaten cold. A few different kinds of cheese. What kind of food would Essie prefer? What did humans normally eat?

If she was already hungry, then it was far too late to send down to the kitchens for anything fancier. Besides, that would mean talking to a servant, then talking to another servant when the food was delivered.

He cut a slice of the bread, then spooned some of the *frishk* onto a plate. Instead of making Essie wait longer, he crossed the room and handed her the plate before he returned to prepare his own lunch.

When he sat on his cushion again with his lunch, he frowned. Essie's plate remained untouched in her hands. Had he done something wrong? "Is it not to your liking?"

She shrugged. "I don't know. I haven't tried it yet. I was waiting for you."

"Why?" Why would she wait? She had been hungry.

"It's considered polite to wait until everyone has their food before you start eating. Is that not how it works here?" Essie filled her fork with *frishk*, then shoved it into her mouth, as if to prove to him that she saw nothing wrong with the food.

"No, we wait for formal meals." He peeked a glance at her before he focused on his own food. "You were hungry. You did not have to wait."

Though, he could not help but feel a little pleased that she had. There was something about eating a meal together. As if they were friends. Or family. Or a true, married couple.

She swallowed and shrugged. "I know."

As they ate, he had to keep his gaze focused on his own plate. Essie shoveled her *frishk* on top of her bread, and the sight sent a crawling feeling along his skin. Food was not supposed to be mixed like that. It was bad enough when food touched on purpose, like in the *frishk*. But mixing food together that was not supposed to be mixed just seemed wrong.

But he was not about to tell her that.

When she set aside her plate, her smile vanished while her posture stiffened.

Not a good sign. What was she going to ask now? Whatever it was, it was not going to be something he would enjoy answering.

Her gaze searched his face. "Why did you agree to this marriage alliance? You didn't have any warning it was coming. I, at least, knew earlier that ending up married to an elf was a possibility, but a marriage alliance to a human wasn't in your plans, I don't think. So why agree to it? More than that, why talk your brother into it?"

Farrendel could not hold her gaze any longer. He could not let her see how desperately he, personally, needed the peace treaty. "My people need peace with your people."

"Yes, I know." She shifted, as if she was trying to figure out how to word her question to get the answer she was looking for. "But why would you agree to a marriage alliance so quickly? You could have tried to talk your brother into marrying one of your sisters to one of my brothers instead. You didn't have to marry me if you hadn't wanted to."

What kind of brother would he have been, if he had tried to foist a marriage of alliance onto one of his sisters instead of taking on the duty himself?

Besides, of all his siblings, he was the most expendable. He was the illegitimate one, after all. "Better me than my sisters."

"I see." Her shoulders slumped, her tone deflating.

He had given the wrong answer and disappointed her somehow. What had Essie expected from him?

She had asked *why*. That was the central question she kept pressing. She was looking for a particular answer, and he kept saying the wrong thing.

He had given her the political answers. Nothing that left him vulnerable.

But she was asking for his personal reasons for marrying her. She wanted something from his heart, not his head.

He forced himself to speak, meeting her gaze. "But not only that."

Her slumped shoulders vanished, her face brightening again.

He had to be honest, no matter how much it hurt. "Your smile. No one else was smiling. They were looking at each other as enemies. But you smiled, as if we were people you were happy to meet."

At his words, she smiled. Bright. Brilliant.

He looked away, even as her smile gave him courage. "I thought that marriage to someone like that would not be miserable."

She placed a hand on one of his. "I hope for much more than not miserable."

"Yes." He croaked out the word. How was he supposed to think when she kept touching him? First his cheek, then his knee, and now his hand. Why did she keep reaching out to him?

Was it possible she had been telling the truth that morning when she said she did not find his scars repulsive?

Ignore the soft feel of her hand against his knuckles. Ignore the way his heart was pounding in his ears. Pretend everything was just fine and normal. He faced her, hoping he appeared nonchalant. "Why did you agree to this arranged marriage?"

She dropped her gaze and her hand from his and instead tugged at the hem of her tunic. "Actually, I kind of suggested it. It started off as a joke, sort of. I was somewhat serious when I said it. Avie decided to use it as an opening gambit, but then you agreed, and I found I was glad you did. Marrying you and coming here has been the best opportunity for an adventure I've ever had."

Adventure. He could pretty much guarantee she would find that.

She gestured around at the room. "And I've always been fascinated by your people and your culture. I read every book our library had on elves. I studied your language as best I could. I can read some elvish, but I can only understand a few spoken words. I'll have to work on that."

"I will help." He found himself saying the words even before he had thought them through. Not that he did not mean them. He did. He just was not used to offering to give of himself so quickly, so easily.

"Thanks." There was her smile again, the one that sent him reeling so much it was a struggle to concentrate as she asked, "What was your plan going into that diplomatic meeting?"

He should smile in return, should he not? That was the socially acceptable thing to do. He made a conscious effort to force his mouth to curve. Hopefully the expression did not look too forced.

What had she asked again? Something about diplomacy? He probably should not tell her. It would let her—and thus her brother—know just how desperate Farrendel and his people were.

But he also could not think of what else to tell her instead. Nor did he want to keep things from her if he could help it. She was so open with him, and it felt like, maybe, they really could make this work if they both had the courage to keep that openness.

He glanced at her, then away. "We planned to agree to almost anything your people suggested. We expected a ceasefire treaty and perhaps an exclusive trade deal. Maybe even exchanging hostages. Marriage was a surprise."

She grinned and leaned forward, almost as if about to touch him again. "Well, let's not tell my brother that. He will be disappointed that he could've gotten peace with a whole lot less than marrying me off. But I'm glad this is the end result."

Farrendel's smile came a little easier this time. If she was glad about this result, if she wanted to make this marriage into something real, then she was hoping for a peace that was more than the mere appeasement that Weylind and Farrendel had been expecting.

Farrendel had hoped to buy his kingdom time. What if he and Essie could do more than that? If he—with her help—could build a lasting peace with Escarland, that would be one less war he would have to fight in the future.

It was a dream he never would have dared contemplate before. It felt dangerous—forbidden, even—to dream. To think about having a future other than fighting and an early death on the battlefield.

But it also seemed like something of which Machasheni Leyleira would approve.

And, perhaps, that was why he even managed to say goodnight to Essie before he fled to his room that night.

CHAPTER
TEN

He had not accidentally killed her when she startled him that morning. That was something. Probably not a good something, all things considered, but Essie had not seemed to be aware of how close he had come to losing control of his magic.

Farrendel strolled next to her through the forest around Ellonahshinel on their way to Estyra.

Essie swayed closer, their shoulders so close they were almost brushing. She peeked up at him. "How is this going to go once we reach Estyra? Are we going to pretend to be a blissfully happy couple? Or walk around like we're still awkward with each other?"

"Elves do not lie." Farrendel could have happily stuffed those words back into his mouth. He had not meant to sound so short. But the panic made him spit out the first thing that came to him.

"It's not a lie. At least, I don't think it is." Essie's gaze swung away from him, the light in her face fading to something more serious. "But there's the truth that you show to other people and the deeper truth that only you know."

He had to concentrate just to keep walking. The deeper truth. Such as the fact that he was shattered inside. The nightmares he was not sure how to explain to her. The shame of his illegitimate birth that he would have to tell Essie eventually and watch the light in her eyes turn into disgust when she looked at him.

He was not ready for that yet. Right now, he simply wanted to enjoy her smiles while he could.

She was smiling at him now. "It's true that, for a marriage of alliance arranged on such short notice, we're doing really well. And I'm optimistic that we will be blissfully happy eventually, considering you find me humorous, and I adore your battle scars. Yes, it's also true that we're still awkward and getting to know each other, and I don't know what you're thinking most of the time, but I'm not sure that is a truth everyone else needs to know. Does that make sense?"

"Yes." Once again the word popped out due to panic more than thought. But her rambling relaxed his tension. "My family will hear about our trip to Estyra."

"Rumors travel fast around here, I take it. It would be best if they believed we are happy. You are happy, right? Or, at least, you said you don't regret marrying me." Essie's scowl flashed across her face so quickly he would have missed it if he had not been watching her. The grimace was replaced with a smaller, more tentative smile as she glanced at him. "In Escarland, a newlywed couple often holds hands in public. It shows everyone they are disgustingly happy together. Do elves hold hands?"

"Yes." He froze. Hold her hand. He could not.

Could he?

Heart pounding so hard it might just tear apart his chest, Farrendel reached for her hand before halting short.

Essie smiled and full-on clasped his hand, their palms together, her fingers wrapping over his knuckles. "This is how we humans hold hands."

His brain was exploding again. He could not breathe. Or think.

He yanked his hand free, gasping in deep breaths as he tried to force his swirling mind to think.

Worse than the panic tightening his chest was the way Essie's face fell, her smile slipping before she managed to hide it. He had hurt her by pulling away. She had been reaching out to him, working to make this relationship real, and he had just shoved her away.

He drew in a shuddery breath and forced himself to move. Hoping she could not tell how his hand trembled, he twined his first two fingers with hers so that the backs of their hands were pressed together. "This is how we elves hold hands."

The grin that lit up Essie's eyes made everything worth it. Her fingers tightened around his, and she stepped still closer, their shoulders brushing. Essie set out walking toward Estyra again, and Farrendel matched her stride.

Their clasped hands swung between them. All he could think about was the warmth of the back of her hand against his. She was so close he caught a whiff of the grass scent of the shampoo he left in the guest room.

He had stocked the room to give an excuse to purchase another set of items from Illyna. He had purposely chosen one of her slowest-selling scents available to help her clear out inventory.

For some reason, the scent did not seem right for Essie. Visiting Illyna's shop would have to be one of the first places he took Essie in Estyra. He had the feeling she would appreciate it. And Illyna would know what would be exactly right for Essie.

As they stepped into Estyra, the relaxed bustle of the town closed around him. His fellow elves strolled along the grass-covered paths around the shops built into the trees. More people wandered along the upper paths formed of branches and swinging bridges.

His breath caught in his chest, and he forced his pace to remain steady. It was not crowded. The people would stare, but they would not bother him. He was fine. He would be fine.

Essie craned her neck, her mouth gaping, as she took everything in.

He might have kept studying her, but a prickling started at the back of his neck. An edginess clawed at his stomach, a wariness deeper than just the staring people.

Farrendel darted a discreet glance around, his gaze skipping past the people sneaking glances at their prince and his new human bride and settling on a flash of familiar chestnut hair.

Iyrinder. Weylind's head bodyguard. He was not even trying to hide his presence. He simply pushed away from the tree where he had been waiting—a place where he would see if Farrendel went to Estyra either by the back way or by the main path from Ellonahshinel—and started following Farrendel and Essie.

Farrendel gritted his teeth, though he kept his expression blank to avoid alerting Essie. Apparently his brother thought Farrendel could not take care of himself. What did Weylind really think would happen? That Essie would attempt to stab him in the back in the middle of the street in broad daylight? Even if Essie had been an assassin—which she certainly was not—no assassin was that foolish.

Apparently, he had been right when he told Essie his family would hear about their trip to Estyra. Not only would they hear about it, but Weylind would get a detailed update from the spy he had set to watch them.

Even knowing the person tailing him was Iyrinder, that itchy feeling at the back of Farrendel's neck did not go away. He kept a wary eye out, but he did not see anyone else who was following him. Though, enough people were staring at him and Essie that it would be hard to pick out someone who was staring for more nefarious purposes than curiosity.

Still, the prickling did not go away while he and Essie ate breakfast or as Farrendel led Essie down the side trail that led to Illyna's shop.

This section of Estyra was quiet. The trees grew closer together. Half of the buildings grown into the trees along here were homes rather than businesses. Fewer elves wandered the trail, while others sat in chairs, reading books or the morning news sheet.

With his fingers still clasped with Essie's, Farrendel led the way up the stairs until they reached Illyna's shop. As they stepped inside, the overwhelming scents flared inside his nose, though his muscles relaxed.

Essie's mouth gaped farther open, her eyes wide as she glanced around at the neat rows of shelves grown into the walls, each shelf filled with jars. Essie spun to him. "Is this...does this shop sell elven shampoo? Like for my hair? Or your hair, I guess. Is this where you get it? Because whatever you use on your hair must be amazing because it's always so perfect. It's probably more elven magic, isn't it?"

Yes, this was the perfect place to bring Essie, based on her excitement.

Illyna hurried from the back room of the shop, her blonde hair floating behind her. As her gaze settled on Farrendel, Essie, then their clasped hands, Illyna's smile twisted with a hint of wariness.

Farrendel braced himself as Illyna stepped toward him. He was not looking forward to having to reassure yet another set of people that Essie was not a danger to him, despite the quick marriage or the fact that she was a human.

Illyna grasped his shoulder with her hand, the stump of her left arm bumping against his shoulder as she spoke in elvish. "It is good to see you are well. You did not seem happy at your wedding. I never would have expected you to leap into marriage like this."

Illyna, Fingol, and the others had been able to sit in the back rows at the wedding. That far back, they would not have been able to see much, nor had they been able to come forward to congratulate Farrendel.

Not to mention, much had changed over the past day thanks to talking to Essie.

"It was a surprise. But not as unwelcome as it might have looked." Farrendel gripped Illyna's shoulder with his free hand, not willing to let go of Essie's hand yet. Something Illyna was sure to notice. He glanced at Essie, still speaking in elvish. "This is my wife, Essie."

Illyna studied Farrendel's face, then turned to Essie.

Farrendel met Essie's gaze and switched to Escarlish. "This is Illyna."

"It is a pleasure to meet you." Illyna faced Essie, going

stiff. "The rumors have been swirling in Estyra about the human princess our Laesornysh brought home."

Farrendel suppressed a sigh. He was inundated with overprotective siblings and friends. Though, he was not too worried about Illyna. She would figure out quickly enough that Essie was not a human to be feared.

"You fought against the trolls, didn't you?" Essie's tone softened.

Illyna darted a glance toward Farrendel, as if asking what he had told Essie. He gave a shrug and a small shake of his head. He had not told Essie anything about Illyna yet, but Essie was very good at reading between the lines. It was one of the things he liked about her. Half the time, she figured out things before he had to come up with the words to explain them.

But he probably should explain a bit more about Illyna. Thanks to his illegitimate birth, the elven court was not above creating salacious rumors about him any time he so much as talked to an unmarried female elf, much less counted them as a friend as he did Illyna.

Would Essie read the wrong thing into his relationship with Illyna? It was strictly friendship. Always had been. They had been bonded by shared experiences, not by any kind of attraction. His grip tightened around Essie's fingers. "She was with the unit who rescued me."

Essie stepped forward. Instead of jealousy, her gaze held a steady openness. "Can I give you a hug? A real, human hug? Because you deserve a hug for helping rescue Farrendel from the trolls."

"A human hug?" Some of the wariness drained from Illyna's shoulders. She shot another glance at Farrendel, and he smiled. It was way too satisfying to watch Essie bewilder someone else for a change.

"Yes. Like this." Releasing Farrendel's hand, Essie wrapped her arms around Illyna in a human hug that was much more gentle than the one he had seen her share with her brothers before they left Escarland.

Over Essie's shoulder, Illyna motioned to Essie, mouthing, "Is she always like this?"

He nodded, and the expression that tugged on his mouth almost felt like a grin. Yes, Essie had won Illyna over just like that. Essie had her own kind of magic. One of warming smiles and infectious joy.

Essie released Illyna after only a moment, as if realizing any more than that would push Illyna's boundaries too far.

Illyna's smile had teasing instead of wariness now, her stance relaxed. "I see the rumors have been wrong. But I should have known. Our Laesornysh does not let people into his life without good reason."

Farrendel's ears burned, and he had to duck his head. What was worse? Having to explain Essie to his wary friends? Or the moment they stopped being wary and started teasing?

"I'm beginning to be really curious about these rumors." Essie clasped her hands in front of her, glancing between Illyna and Farrendel as if hoping one of them would tell her.

Farrendel could not meet her gaze. He had yet to hear the rumors, but he could guess. Probably something along the lines of how the illegitimate prince could not help but cause more scandal by marrying a human. Or how if one of the elven royalty had to be sacrificed, it might as well be the prince whose blood was already tainted.

"I am sure you are." Illyna's tone gave nothing away.

Instead, she gestured at her shop, with a smile. "But you are not here to trade gossip. You are here for some of my products."

That brought the smile back to Essie's face. "What do you have for shampoo?" She dropped her gaze almost immediately. "Not that I need anything. The shampoo I was given will work fine."

There was something to her tone of voice that itched at him. He opened his mouth, trying to think of what to tell her. This was her home now. She should feel free to pick out something as simple as new shampoo and conditioner without worry about what he would think.

Illyna stepped in before he managed to get a word out. She sniffed a lock of Essie's hair, grimacing. "No, it will not. Basic grass is a perfectly reasonable scent to keep on hand for guests when you want a generic smell, but it is not suitable for a princess."

He could hear Illyna's teasing reprimand, and he winced. If he had had time to better prepare for getting married, he would have replaced that awful grass shampoo before bringing Essie home. Perhaps, if he had been less panicked by everything, he would have thought to send a message to Illyna to prepare the guest room for Essie.

Too late now.

Illyna sent him a look that all but ordered him to leave. "Farrendel, unless you need anything, you might wish to step out and come back in an hour or so."

For a moment, he hesitated. Should he leave Essie alone with Illyna? It was not like Illyna would hurt Essie. But she was bound to low-key interrogate her, given the chance.

But Essie willingly fell into step with Illyna, her gaze already focused on the rows upon rows of jars.

She would be fine. And Farrendel would not mind a few minutes to himself to work through everything that had happened over the past few days.

Farrendel quietly slipped out of the door to Illyna's shop and drew in a deep breath in the silence that closed around him. That silence was welcome, and yet he strangely missed Essie's chatter at the same time.

Iyrinder waited at the bottom of the stairs to Illyna's shop, leaning against the tree's broad trunk and not even trying to hide the fact that he was waiting for Farrendel. Farther down the path, Fingol and his wife, two of Farrendel's friends, were loitering near one of the shops, also waiting.

Farrendel suppressed a sigh as he strode down the stairs and halted in front of Iyrinder. "You can tell my brother that I do not need a babysitter."

Iyrinder's mouth quirked in the hint of a smile. "I already did, in a very respectful and tactful manner, but there is not much I can say when I am given an order by my king."

True. While Farrendel had the luxury of talking back to Weylind about his hovering, Iyrinder did not. "What will you tell him when you make your report?"

Iyrinder's smile curved wider. "I will tell him that Prince Farrendel and his human princess seem to be happy together, and that Princess Elspeth has been genuinely kind to all the elves she has met."

Farrendel relaxed and shook his head. "He will not believe you."

"He cannot blame me if he does not like what I have to report." Iyrinder shrugged.

There was a reason Farrendel liked working with him, even if he ultimately answered to Weylind.

Farrendel glanced toward Fingol and Fydella, who had edged closer while he had been talking with Iyrinder. Like Illyna, they would be curious about Essie.

Turning back to Iyrinder, Farrendel gestured toward Illyna's shop. "Could you please guard Princess Elspeth while I am gone?"

After all, if Iyrinder was here, then Farrendel might as well make use of him. Turn the annoyance into an asset.

As if knowing exactly what Farrendel was thinking, Iyrinder gave another wry smile. "I have technically been ordered to keep an eye on Princess Elspeth. I would be derelict in my duties if I did otherwise."

Good. Iyrinder would keep Essie safe, even if he had not come right out and said it. That itchy feeling had gone away, but Farrendel could not afford to let his guard down completely. There were enough people in Estyra who did not like humans and might take the opportunity to hurt Essie if given the chance.

With Iyrinder guarding Essie, Farrendel was free to stroll down the street.

While Fydella hung back, Fingol strode to meet him, limping only a little on the leg he had permanently injured in battle. He raised his eyebrows as he studied Farrendel. "You seem happier than you were at your wedding."

Farrendel ducked his head, struggling to put into words what exactly had changed between the time he had married Essie to now.

They had talked. She had not flinched away from his scars, but instead had talked several times about making this marriage into something real and lasting and good.

If he was going to make this marriage real, then Farrendel needed advice. He was not about to ask Weylind. Weylind was too grumpy about this whole arranged marriage thing. Machasheni Leyleira had already given her advice, cryptic as it had been.

But Farrendel needed practical advice, and Fingol happened to be the only married friend he had.

"How..." Farrendel could not meet Fingol's gaze and instead gazed at the sky, the branches overhead, the grass covering the ground. "How do you actually go about falling in love?"

Fingol made a choking cough. "Pardon?"

Farrendel opened and shut his mouth, his head buzzing. He had to somehow spit out the words from the jumble in his head. He waved from Fingol to Fydella and back. "You are married. You fell in love. How did you do it?"

Shaking his head, Fingol shifted, not looking at Farrendel. "Can you not ask your brother?"

For a moment, all Farrendel could do was gesture wordlessly. What could he say? While Fingol was a friend, Farrendel still could not disparage Weylind. Finally, Farrendel shook his head. "No, I cannot."

"I...see." Fingol sighed, lines creasing his face as if he was facing a battle rather than a mere conversation.

Farrendel's ears burned. He should not have opened his mouth. What had he been thinking, asking Fingol such a personal question? "Forget I said anything."

Fingol heaved a sigh. "No, no. You clearly need advice. Come. Let us get a quiet table at a café where we can talk."

"I cannot leave..." Farrendel waved in the direction of Illyna's shop where Essie was.

"We will not go far." Fingol led the way to his wife Fydella, where he leaned close for a whispered conversation.

Farrendel shifted from foot to foot. He still had time. He could make a run for it. Perhaps return to Illyna's shop and hide there for a while until Fingol forgot that he had ever brought up this topic.

The longer the whispered conversation continued, the wider Fydella's grin grew until she turned to Farrendel. "Yes, let us sit and talk."

Fydella led the way at a brisk pace to a nearby café. It was owned by another elf warrior who had fought with Fingol and Farrendel before he was wounded.

Fingol and Fydella claimed a quiet table tucked under a sapling at the far side of the café, well away from any other patrons. While Fingol and Farrendel hesitated, Fydella rolled her eyes and took the seat with her back to the rest of the café.

After a moment of silent staring, Fingol caved first and claimed the chair that placed his back to the empty forest, leaving the seat with its back safely protected by the sapling for Farrendel.

Farrendel took a deep breath and forced himself to sit. Why had he opened his mouth? He should have just stayed quiet. When he stayed quiet, he did not say anything he later regretted. And this debacle was one that would come back to haunt him for *years*.

He glanced around the café. Only a few others sat at the tables at this time in the morning, and none of them were close enough to overhear. The nearest was an elf reading a book, his head down. A cane rested against the table next to him. Farrendel vaguely recognized him as a wounded elf warrior who worked for one of Weylind's generals, though Farrendel had never had the opportunity to strike up a friendship with him the way he had with Illyna or Fingol. Not likely to be a threat.

An elf server came and took their orders. They waited in a long, awkward silence for the server to return with their cups of tea.

When the server set Farrendel's cup in front of him, he stirred in lots of the provided milk and sugar. He didn't actually like tea, but the ubiquitous drink was a social ritual here in Tarenhiel. He had no choice but to drink it. At least the milk and sugar made it somewhat palatable.

Fingol leaned forward. "So...falling in love."

This had been such a bad idea. Farrendel lifted his cup and took a sip to buy himself time. It took all his practice at holding an icy mask to keep the grimace off his face. Even with the milk and sugar, the tea still tasted like bitter, hot water.

Fydella smiled and sipped her own tea. "Why don't you start by telling us about this human princess you married? Perhaps then we might be able to pinpoint something specific that would help."

Good. A topic to focus on. Farrendel set down his teacup and stared at it as he relayed the events of his marriage to Princess Elspeth. He left out anything of the treaty negotiations that would be considered confidential and instead focused on Essie.

"And then...and then this morning, she wanted to *hold my hand*." Farrendel slumped against the back of his chair, strangely wrung out after so much talking, even if it was with his friends.

"Yes. We noticed." Fingol gave a wry smile.

Fydella's mouth also tipped into a smile. "Farrendel

Amir, wanting to hold your hand is a *good* thing. Forgive me for being blunt, but I do not see the problem?"

Farrendel heaved a frustrated sigh. His words were not working. How could he communicate the roil inside him? "That *is* the problem! If she just wanted to ignore me, I could do that. I am good at ignoring people. But she wants...more. And I do not know what to do or say or..." He gestured, his words failing.

Fingol gave a small cough. "Are you attracted to her?"

Was he? Farrendel squeezed his eyes shut for a moment, drawing in a deep and steadying breath. He thought of Essie's smile and the way it sparkled in her eyes and lit her expression. The way her red hair glowed in the morning sunlight. Her never-ending chatter that, for some reason, relaxed his tension rather than added to it.

And, in the end, the answer was simple. "Yes."

"Ah." Fingol shared a look with Fydella. Based on the angle of their arms, they were holding hands beneath the table. "If I understand this correctly, your problem is that you went into this marriage expecting that the two of you would just coldly ignore each other. But now that you are married, you find you are attracted to her and she seems to be attracted to you, and you actually want to build a true marriage. Does that sum it up?"

"*Yes.*" That was what Farrendel had been trying to say, but Fingol had said it all so much better.

"If that is what you want, then as far as I can see, you are making a good start of it." Fingol waved in the direction of Illyna's shop. "You are spending time with her. You are talking and listening. From here, you take that attraction and build it into something deeper and meaningful."

Farrendel gritted his teeth. But how? How did he go from mere attraction into something more? Just time? And talking? Surely there was something else to it, right? It seemed too…simple.

Fydella set aside her empty teacup and held Farrendel's gaze with a gentle, compassionate expression. "You will need to take the time to truly listen to her. Right now, you are still getting to know each other. You are learning the surface things. As you spend more time together, you will learn the deeper truths about each other. You will both need to be vulnerable and open."

Farrendel nodded, even as his chest tightened. Open and vulnerable was not something he did. Ever. If he was vulnerable, then he could be hurt.

Apparently this was not so simple after all. Spending time with Essie was easy. Even talking with her was mostly easy.

But truly opening up in a way where his heart could actually be hurt? That was much, much harder.

Fingol leaned a little closer to his wife. "You need to be concerned about her needs and not just your own. It means you will need to make changes, and I know how difficult that is for you."

Now Farrendel was struggling to keep his breathing even past the rising tension inside his chest. Could he even change? Change was bad. Change messed with his head until he could not think straight. Change meant venturing out of the safe routines into something that could send him tumbling.

"Farrendel, amir." Fydella's voice remained gentle, and yet was firm enough to yank him from his spiraling thoughts. She gave him another one of those sympathetic smiles. "Take it one step at a time. You are already married, and that means you both were thrown into the deep side of the pond right away. But you can still take your time and build a relationship that is strong and lasting."

One step at a time. He could do that. Right?

"What we are trying to say is that it looks like you are taking the right steps." Fingol shook his head. "Perhaps you needed some advice. But all you really needed was someone to tell you that you are doing things right."

That eased some of the tension twisting Farrendel's throat. He gave a small nod. "Linshi."

Fingol gave a sigh and slumped against the back of his seat, as if relieved to get that conversation over with.

Farrendel could not blame him. He was relieved it was over as well.

But, uncomfortable as it had been, Fingol and Fydella had been helpful. Now Farrendel could formulate a battle plan and approach this with some strategy instead of flailing about in panic.

ELEVEN

F arrendel held Essie's hand as they strolled from the lift back to his suite of rooms.

No, *their* suite of rooms. He was not quite sure when that had changed, but Essie seemed to belong here. With her at his side, the world was painted in brighter colors. Especially when she smiled.

Yet, as he neared the main room, something tugged at his senses. He froze so quickly that Essie ran into him.

Her grip on his hand tightened as she remained tucked behind him, as if instinctively seeking safety in his presence. "What is it?"

"Someone is inside." He reached out with his magical senses, searching for danger. Instead of danger, he recognized something even worse. "My brother."

Essie stiffened as well, and he could not blame her. Weylind had been particularly grumpy lately.

Not to mention that if Weylind was here, a mere two days after Farrendel's wedding, then it could not be for a good reason.

Even knowing Weylind was waiting inside for them, Farrendel kept his firm grip on Essie's hand. Let Weylind see and get even more grumpy. Farrendel did not care.

He strode into the room and spat the word to turn the lights on, because of course Weylind was dramatically waiting around in the dark for them.

As the lights flared on, Farrendel spotted Weylind. He had been sprawled on the cushions on the far side of the room, all of his limbs stiff, his gaze hard.

"What are you doing here, Weylind?" Farrendel did not try to keep the bite out of his voice. Weylind had always been a little overprotective, but he had turned downright smothering lately. He had sent Iyrinder to spy on Farrendel and Essie. And if he was here merely to hover, then Farrendel might be tempted to show him out the door with a little bit of magic to help him hurry on his way.

Yet, as Weylind stood with a heaviness slumping his shoulders and slowing his motion, Farrendel's stomach tightened. This was not about Weylind's hovering, even if Weylind's gaze hardened at the sight of Farrendel holding Essie's hand.

Farrendel tugged Essie closer, his chest squeezing until he could barely force the words out. "What is it?"

Weylind's gaze swerved away from Farrendel, sighing. "There has been a raid on one of our border encampments, and the troll raiding party has remained just over the border."

Which meant both that the troll army was planning another raid and that they were within striking distance, if the elven army had Farrendel reinforcing them.

Farrendel wanted to pull Essie closer. He wanted to

stay here with her where everything was bright and warm.

But he could not. It was his duty to defend Tarenhiel. If he did not fight, then other elven warriors would have to do so. Warriors who did not have his magic and who would die in the fighting.

He drew in a deep breath and faced Weylind. "When do we leave?"

"Tonight." Weylind strode past him, then halted for just a moment to meet Farrendel's gaze. "I am sorry."

As the door clicked shut behind Weylind, Farrendel let go of Essie's hand, her warm fingers sliding free and leaving his hand so very cold and empty.

The last two days had been golden and beautiful. But, as always, such a life was not Farrendel's. No, he had been born for bloodshed and war, as was proved by the terrible magic flowing through his veins.

Essie glanced from the door to Farrendel, then reached out to grip his arm. "What happened? What did he say?"

Ice settled into Farrendel's chest. Already, he was mentally pulling away from Essie's warmth and happiness and, instead, clung to the cold he would need when he faced the troll army camped at Tarenhiel's border. "Trolls have raided the border. The border guards have asked for my help to end the raids."

Essie's face twisted, her eyes widening, for just a moment before her expression smoothed into that composed, perfect princess look he had seen when he first married her. "When do you leave?"

"Tonight." It was hard to even get that one word out. Now that he had been summoned, all he wanted to do was grab his things and leave. Dragging this out would just make it harder to hold onto the cold inside him.

As if sensing the churning inside him, Essie lifted her chin, resolve glowing in her green eyes. "Don't worry about me. I'll be fine here. Just stay safe and come back to me, all right?"

It was cruel, leaving her here alone in a foreign kingdom. Perhaps he should have taken the time to introduce her to his family properly so that she would at least have someone to look after her instead of keeping her so much to himself for the past two days.

But Farrendel had no choice. And if anyone could land on her feet and survive here in Tarenhiel, it was Essie.

He forced himself to turn around and walk away from her, each step growing harder.

At the door, he halted, his feet frozen. Everything in him churned, rebelling at the thought of just leaving her like this.

If only he was not Laesornysh. If only he could simply be Prince Farrendel, enjoying Essie's company and experiencing the peace found in Estyra, far away from the border with Kostaria.

He half-turned, glancing over his shoulder at Essie. She hugged her arms over her stomach, her composed expression slipping.

She was cut off from her kingdom, her friends, her family. The least he could do was offer her something, anything, to make her feel less alone. "If you want to write a quick note for your family, I will make sure it is sent before I leave."

He could not bear to hold her gaze. It hurt too much as it clashed against the ice in his heart.

Instead, he turned and retreated up the stairs to his

room. By habit, he changed into the black trousers and green tunic he wore underneath his fighting leathers. Those fighting leathers were already in a trunk on the train, waiting for his next battle. All he had to do was gather his weapons, and he was ready to go to war once again.

He was Laesornysh. Death on the Wind. He did not have the luxury to experience happiness or smiles or anything approaching a normal life.

Essie might enjoy his company now, but how would she react when he returned from the battles and his nightmares struck in full force? There would be no hiding them. Once Essie realized what he truly was, then she would hate him. This camaraderie between them would end once and for all.

What else had he expected? He was Laesornysh. The illegitimate son of the elf king, cursed with terrible, deadly magic.

When he re-entered the main room, Essie was sealing her letter with wax. With wide eyes, she held out her letter, a white look to her face. "I kept it short."

The cold settled even deeper in Farrendel's chest and veins. With his black clothing and weapons, he was scaring her.

If he was scaring her now, then she would be terrified if she found out what he could do.

The last few days had been wonderful. But of course they had to end.

Farrendel took the letter and forced himself to stride past her. He could not pause. He could not give in to the temptation to ease his hold on the ice.

"Farrendel?"

Essie's voice was soft, yet it still had the power to halt

his feet. It took all the courage in him to glance over his shoulder at her.

"Stay safe." Essie's large green eyes held his gaze. "I thought you should know. I'll miss you."

If she kept looking at him like that, then he would crumble. He didn't have the strength to deal with what she was offering him.

Hope. Life. Happiness.

None of those things would ever belong to him. And the quicker he accepted that, the better.

Clinging to all the hardness he could muster, Farrendel turned his back to her and strode out the door.

At this late hour, the pathways of Ellonahshinel were deserted. Farrendel strode over the branches swiftly, gripping Essie's letter, until he reached Weylind's study near the center of the large treetop palace.

Here, the branches weren't deserted. Instead, aides and servants bustled back and forth as they prepared for the king's late-night departure. Weylind stood next to his desk, hunching as he swiftly signed paper after paper to get through a week's worth of paperwork in a few minutes.

Farrendel had to press his back to the wall and edge through the doorway past an aide to enter the room. His throat closed at the presence of so many people packed into a tiny space. If he did not have Essie's letter burning against his fingers, he would bolt for the train.

Weylind glanced up, then he straightened. "Farrendel. Was there something you needed before we leave?"

Too many people. Farrendel swallowed several times, the words sticking in the back of his throat.

Weylind glanced from him to the aides who had frozen where they stood, shifting as if they did not want to be in the same room as Farrendel. With a flick of his hand, Weylind dismissed them.

The aides hurried from the room, piling through the doorway in a way that was verging on undignified.

When it was just him and Weylind left in the room, Farrendel took a deep breath and held out the letter. "I have a letter from Essie—Princess Elspeth—that needs to be sent to Escarland."

Weylind's jaw did not harden, exactly. But something flashed in his eyes as he pointed to an empty spot on his desk. "I will leave instructions for it to be sent in the morning after someone has had a chance to look it over for any sensitive information the human princess might try to send back to her brother."

Wait, Weylind intended to have someone read Essie's letter? Farrendel's fingers tightened over the piece of paper. Sure, she was a princess of an enemy kingdom. Perhaps she was even a spy, as Weylind had maintained since the diplomatic meeting.

But it still seemed wrong to let one of Weylind's aides paw through her letter. These words were meant for her family. No one else.

Farrendel glanced down at the letter he held. Essie had sealed it, but she had used only a small glob of wax and had pressed it flat without any identifying marks, even though she was sure to have a royal seal along. It was almost as if she expected that her letter would be read before it was sent to Escarland.

He was too broken to give her happiness or love. But he could give her protection here in Tarenhiel, even if that meant protecting her from his own family.

As Weylind reached for the letter, Farrendel snatched it back. Ignoring the puzzled furrow to Weylind's brow,

Farrendel marched around Weylind's desk, snatched Weylind's seal from the top of the desk, and pressed it into the still-warm glob of wax. It did not work quite as well as it would have with fresh wax, but it was still distinctive enough for everyone to recognize the king's seal.

Yes, it was a crime for anyone but Weylind to use the king's seal. But Farrendel and Weylind were alone, and Weylind was not about to do anything to Farrendel.

Farrendel would have used his own seal, but he had left it back in his rooms. He rarely had any reason to use it.

Besides, Weylind's seal was better, in the end. An overzealous border guard might still dare to break Farrendel's seal, but no one, at least on the Tarenhieli side of the border, would break the king's seal, even on a letter going to Escarland.

Farrendel faced Weylind and held out the letter again. "This needs to be sent to King Averett of Escarland."

Weylind's jaw was definitely flexing now. "Shashon, what are you doing? We do not know what information about you or Tarenhiel she might send to her brother."

"She is no spy." Farrendel held Weylind's gaze. He was not going to back down on this. "This is a letter to her family. No one else will read it, understand? If that creates trouble for Tarenhiel, it will be on my head."

"A little late for that now that you have used my seal on it," Weylind muttered. After a pause, he raised his voice, calling for one of his clerks.

A clerk hurried inside. "What do you need, Daresheni?"

Weylind gestured to the letter Farrendel held. "Please

see to it that this letter is sent to Escarland as soon as possible."

The clerk's eyes widened, but she took the letter from Farrendel. "I will see to it, Daresheni."

As the aide turned to leave, Weylind raised an eyebrow at Farrendel, as if asking, *Are you happy now?*

Farrendel gave a short nod and turned toward the door.

"Shashon?" Weylind's voice halted Farrendel at the door. "If you wish to talk...I know these last few days have been tumultuous..."

Farrendel spun on his heel, gritting his teeth to keep from yelling at his brother. Really? Weylind was offering to talk? Now? As if Farrendel wanted to talk about Essie with Weylind after Weylind had become smothering. "Only if you want to talk about how you sent Iyrinder to spy on me and Essie."

Weylind gave a slight cough. "I will meet you on the train."

That was what Farrendel thought. He turned on his heel once again and left.

He boarded the train and locked himself in his private car to wait out the nearly sleepless night as the train glided toward the border with Kostaria. It was as if Essie and the brief glimpse of happiness that she had given him had never existed.

CHAPTER
TWELVE

F arrendel crouched in the brush at the edge of the Gulmorth Gorge. Far below, the Gulmorth River surged between the two, sharp cliff faces formed of hard granite.

Somewhere on the far side of the gorge, the troll army remained hidden in the jumble of rocks and tall pine trees.

No matter how well their army was currently hidden, the troll warriors would fall to Farrendel's magic as soon as Weylind and the rest of the elven army flushed them out.

A small squad of warriors crouched in the brush behind Farrendel. Weylind had insisted, of course. He was not going to send Farrendel off on his own, even if Farrendel now had an entire squad he had to worry about accidentally killing.

The commander eased into the stand of trees next to Farrendel. The smile the commander sent Farrendel was far too reverent. "It is a pleasure to go into battle with you, Laesornysh. My warriors and I will guard your back."

Farrendel froze, trying to process those words and come up with a socially accepted response. At least with the nobility's dislike, all he had to do was put on his hard Laesornysh face. But this awe from those in the army? That was harder to handle.

After a long moment, he managed a nod.

It seemed to satisfy the warrior. He gave an even more enthusiastic nod in return, then faced forward once again, studying the Kostarian side of the gorge.

Farrendel checked his swords in their sheaths on his back. The back sheaths were more cumbersome for drawing his short swords. But the back sheaths kept the leather out of his way while he was fighting and flipping, and the swords were more secure there than on his hip while climbing.

A blast of plant growing magic flared to their right, just out of sight behind an outcropping. Roots reached for the far side of the gorge.

Stone and ice blasted from the far side, followed by the hooting war chants of the trolls, though they remained concealed.

With a few whispered words, the commander motioned to his squad. Two elves crept forward and unrolled rope ladders down the side of the cliffs. Half the squad swarmed down the ladders, then it was Farrendel's turn. He checked his swords one last time before he climbed over the side of the cliff and quickly navigated down the rope ladder.

By the time his boots landed on the small ledge of stone next to the raging Gulmorth River, the members of the squad tossed grappling hooks, snagging them in the tumbles of rocks at the top of the far side. The first two swung across, landing on the far side of the Gulmorth. They tossed the ropes back and stepped aside as two more elves swung across.

Farrendel caught a rope and swung across, landing lightly. The sounds of fighting echoed down the Gulmorth Gorge as Weylind and the rest of the army battled the trolls across the way.

Once the rest of the squad had crossed, Farrendel pushed past the others to grab one of the ropes.

The commander opened his mouth, as if he wanted to protest. But after a moment, he nodded and gripped the other rope.

With one last deep breath, Farrendel drew on the ice in his chest, in his veins. He climbed the rope hand over hand, then rolled onto the ground above, coming up in a crouch. Drawing his swords, he crept through the rocks, circling farther around where the trolls seemed to be hiding. He did not wait for the squad to climb the ropes. They were not necessary, not for his style of fighting. They were only there to appease Weylind's overprotectiveness.

With ice still filling his veins, Farrendel drew on his magic, letting bolts twine around his fingers. The rest of his magic tugged at his control, begging to be unleashed, eager to destroy and kill.

Farrendel gritted his teeth and held most of his magic in check. He did not dare let it blast out as it wished.

Arrows and bullets pelted against the fringe of his magic. He let just a little more of his magic blast around him as he leapt onto the rocks, charging at the hiding trolls.

Troll warriors turned to face him, raising swords and

axes. Farrendel stabbed down at one troll, taking him through the chest. He pushed away and parried another troll's sword. He coated his swords with magic and plunged into the mass of troll warriors. His magic blasted around him, killing even more trolls than he killed with his swords.

A roar from his left drew his attention. A second army of troll warriors charged from the rocks and stands of trees deeper into Kostaria.

Farrendel pivoted, placing his back to the gorge behind him. This had been a trap. For him. The trolls had lured him across the gorge and now they had him pinned between two squads of this raiding party.

It did not matter. These squads would simply be more trolls for him to kill.

What would Essie think if she saw him now? Spattered in blood and about to massacre all these troll warriors in front of him.

No, he could not think about Essie. Not now.

He needed to be cold as the stone around him, all the way to his heart.

More of his magic burst past his control, and he scrambled to direct it at the charging trolls.

A wall of ice sprang up between him and the trolls, taking the brunt of his power.

He had to unleash more of his magic. Behind him, the members of the squad crouched, depending on him—on his magic—to keep them alive.

More magic. More death. Farrendel's magic burned through his fingers as he released as little as possible.

Killing. Killing. Blood flowing over the stone beneath his feet, coating his clothes, his hair. Until the trolls finally retreated, and Farrendel could finally clamp down on his magic once again.

When he could finally retreat back across the Gulmorth, he ignored the cheers of *Laesornysh* that followed him as he walked between the shelters of the encampment. He did not want their praise for this. Not for the blood he carried on his hands.

Weylind approached, but Farrendel stalked past him with a nod, not wanting to talk. Brushing past Weylind, Farrendel climbed the short ladder, then into his shelter in the tree next to Weylind's.

Inside, he found a bucket of water and rags waiting for him. Weylind, looking out for him.

Farrendel peeled off his bloody clothes, then washed as best he could with the bucket and rags until the water sloshing in the bucket was a deep, bright red.

So much blood. None of it his own.

Farrendel did not have to imagine what Essie would think of him. She was all light and happiness. If she could see him now, she would turn away in disgust.

AFTER FIVE DAYS OF FIGHTING—AND killing—at the border, Farrendel was worn thin. He straightened his private train car, taking his time packing his few things that he would take with him back to his rooms in Ellonahshinel. Even after his delays, he still found Weylind on the train platform, waiting for him, the sunset glinting on his black hair.

Farrendel ducked his head and lengthened his stride, trying to brush past his brother. He did not want to talk. He was holding himself together with shaking threads.

The pressure of trying to talk with Weylind—of deflecting his queries—might be too much. Would be too much.

Instead, Weylind fell into step with him, matching his pace. "That human princess will be in your rooms."

Farrendel's stride hitched, but he refused to give Weylind more of a reaction than that unintentional one.

Not just a random human princess. His wife. Essie.

Would she be waiting for him? A part of him desperately needed to see her and bask in the warmth of her smile until he felt alive again instead of this hollowed out shell. But another part of him was too weary to handle anyone, even her. He did not want her to see him like this. All he wanted to do was shut his door—shut everyone out—and just *survive* another day.

Weylind glanced at him, gaze searching Farrendel's face. "There are plenty of rooms on the family branch. You can stay there tonight if you wish."

Farrendel could hear what Weylind was not saying. He was asking if Farrendel would move back to the family branch, a place he had abandoned for his far-flung set of rooms fifteen years ago.

But he could not do that. Not when his family would suffocate him trying to help. Not when he would certainly cry out in his nightmares tonight.

His blood ran cold, and he nearly stopped dead in his tracks again. If he had nightmares tonight, Essie would hear. Would he frighten her?

Perhaps he should take Weylind up on his offer, just this once. Or better yet, stay in his private train car until the nightmares were spent in a few days or a week.

Yet that would leave Essie on her own for longer. And he could not do that to her. They had been married all of three days before he had left for a week of war.

Weylind was still casting glances at Farrendel, waiting for an answer.

"I will be fine." Farrendel worked to keep his tone cold. If he showed just how shattered he was, Weylind might take matters into his own hands.

Weylind's gaze searched his face, as if he did not believe Farrendel's assertion. But, thankfully, they reached the stairs to Ellonahshinel and joined the bustle of servants, warriors, and nobles going to and from the treetop palace. Weylind was caught up by several of the nobles, and Farrendel quickly slipped away from the conversation. A few people nodded to him or welcomed him back, but his expression must have been forbidding enough that most people left him alone.

As he neared his rooms, his heart beat harder. Would Essie greet him? He had never had anyone waiting for him to return, not like this. Sure, his family waited for him to return from war, but it was different to think about a *wife* waiting for him.

Yet when he reached his suite of rooms, all of them were dark. As he pushed open the door to the main room, he could sense the emptiness. Not just of this main room, but all the rooms of his suite.

Where was Essie? Where would she go? It was not like he had given her much of a tour before he had left.

Though, he had been gone a week. While he would have huddled in his rooms avoiding everyone if he had been in Essie's place, she likely would not have done so.

He shut the door and sagged against it, his heart sinking. It was not like he had expected Essie to be here to greet him with a warm smile but...he had deep down been hoping for that. It left him empty to find the rooms just as cold and lonely as they always were when he returned.

Pushing off from the door, he dragged himself up the stairs to his own room, shutting and locking that door behind him. He showered and dressed in comfortable clothes before he sat on his bed, leaning against the wall.

How long he sat there in his dark room, staring at nothing, trying to think about nothing, he did not know. The forest outside his window turned gray, then darkened into night. He could hear the opening and closing of doors when Essie returned from wherever she had been. Essie's footsteps scuffed on the stairs to her room before her door shut.

He did not dare let himself sleep. If he dreamed—if he cried out in his nightmares—he would scare Essie.

Instead, he sat there, staring into the darkness.

HE MUST HAVE FALLEN ASLEEP. He woke from his own scream in his nightmare, his throat raw, his tongue gummy in his mouth.

For long minutes, he curled on his bed, struggling to pull himself from the fog of his nightmares. He fisted his shaking hands in his blankets below him and told himself to breathe deeply and evenly. He was alive. He was not being tortured. He was safe.

Distantly, he registered the sounds of doors softly opening and closing, accompanied by Essie's footsteps. He stilled as he heard her footsteps on the steps to his room moments before a light knock rapped against his door.

What was he supposed to do? He did not want Essie to see him like…this.

After several moments of silence, she knocked again, this time calling out quietly, "Farrendel?"

She was not going to leave. And, suddenly, he did not want her to go. He wanted—needed—a glimpse of her smile to remind him of light and happiness to get himself through tonight.

He rolled to his feet, crept across the room, and opened the door, bracing himself against the doorjamb to hide his shaking.

Essie stood there, her eyes shining in the starlight as she flicked a glance at him before looking down. "Your brother said to give you space, and I was going to, but you cried out in your sleep loud enough I could hear it in my room, and I wanted to make sure you were all right and if I could do anything to help, even if it's just sit with you for a while if you don't want to go to sleep again right away. But if you want space, that's fine too. I'll go back to my room and let you have space if that's what you need right now. I understand."

She cared. He froze, not sure how to respond to so many words coming at him at this time of night. Even after hearing his scream in the night, she had still come here to try to comfort him.

She peeked at him again, her mouth tilting with an expression he could not read, and she shifted closer. "Would it be all right if I hugged you?"

Hug him? The way she had Illyna?

He could not breathe. Could not move. Could not think.

Yet, for some inexplicable reason, he found himself tilting his head in a stiff nod.

She stepped closer, then eased her arms around him. Her hands rested against his back a moment before she leaned her head against his chest.

His breath caught. She was so soft and warm against him. She made him want to gather her in his arms and hold her close. Bury his face against her hair and drink in her presence.

But he could not bring himself to act on those impulses. He was not yet ready to embrace her as she was embracing him. She trusted him, strange as it seemed. And he trusted her. At least, he wanted to trust her.

"I missed you while you were gone," Essie mumbled against his shirt.

He released a breath, the tension in his muscles easing for the first time since his nightmare. He was not sure what it was about Essie that relaxed him in a way no one else did. She seemed to have so little anxiety that it eased his anxiety.

After another moment, Essie pulled back, though she rested a hand on his chest as if to keep him connected to her. "I don't know all your reasons for asking your family to give you space after a battle like this, but I understand there are some parts of ourselves that we can't show even our families. But you don't have to hide anything from me."

What would it be like, not hiding? He was not sure if he could. There was so much that she did not yet know. She did not know he was illegitimate. She did not know about the torture he had suffered, the trolls he had killed, what he saw in his nightmares.

Perhaps someday he would tell her. But not now. Not tonight, with this nightmare so raw in his mind.

Essie's gaze searched his face. "I don't fully understand all the implications of the elven marriage vows we spoke, but they are similar enough to the human ones that I know that in marriage our hearts are linked. That means when you are hurting, I'm hurting. When you need help, I'm here to help. If you want space, I'll give you space. But please know you don't have to be alone. I'm here for you."

She was asking him for a response. Words. He needed words. She had talked. Hugged him. And he had yet to even indicate that he appreciated what she was doing.

Drawing in a shaky breath, he reached with trembling fingers and, feeling bold, he clasped her hand. When she did not pull away, he met her gaze. "Do not leave."

For a moment, she blinked at him. Then her smile lit her face as she squeezed his hand. "Why don't we go to the main room and just talk for a while?"

That sounded all right by him. He managed another nod, and then he let Essie tug him down his stairs and into the main room.

When they entered the room, Essie let go of his hand and bustled toward the cold cupboard, navigating the room confidently even in the dark. "Would you like a drink? Water? Juice?"

"Water." His throat scratched after his screams in his nightmare.

While Essie moved about the kitchen, he settled onto the lounging cushions on the floor, leaning against the wall and drawing his knees up. Just the walk from his room to here felt exhausting. Not physically, yet a heavy weariness pressed down on him.

She crossed the room and held out a cup of water. As soon as he took it, she hurried across the room and pulled out two blankets. When she returned to his side, she set one blanket next to him and kept the other for herself. She settled onto a cushion next to him. Not touching, but close enough for him to still sense her warmth and presence.

He sipped the cold water, trying to gather the shreds of his composure. Would she ask about his nightmare? What would he say if she did?

Instead, she began talking about dining with his family, spending time with Machasheni Leyleira and Illyna, and ideas for the future. Her chatter relaxed his muscles even more until he found himself responding and asking questions.

At some point, Essie's words trailed off, and she curled on the cushions underneath her blanket. Her breathing deepened, and soon she was making soft whuffling sounds in her sleep.

Farrendel set his cup aside, spread out the blanket she had given him, and curled on the cushions within arm's reach of Essie. When he fell asleep this time, he did not dream.

WHEN HE WOKE, Essie still slept on her pile of cushions, her breathing deep and even.

He smiled and let his eyes fall closed again, enjoying the feeling of restfulness on a night when he had expected nothing but nightmares.

She had not flinched away from him last night. Despite his nightmares, his silence, his tension, she had stuck by him. There was just something about her chatter and her smiles that was strangely restful and calmed him in a way that none of his family members had ever managed to do. Their anxious worry for him just added to his own tension instead of diffusing it the way Essie did with her calm acceptance.

It was probably a little soon to be falling in love with her. And he did not know exactly what falling in love felt like.

But this feeling in his chest—the warmth, the draw to Essie, the need to spend time with her and care for her—seemed a lot like love to him.

THIRTEEN

Dinner with his family had gone as well as could be expected. They had been surprised that Farrendel had shown up. Even more surprised that he and Essie were dressed up and wearing crowns, making a statement that they were united.

But dinner had reminded him that Essie had only limited knowledge of elvish. It was time he started teaching her, if she wished to learn. He did not mind translating for her, but he would be called away to war again before long.

After exercising, he hurried through his shower and reached the main room. As he heard noise from Essie's room, he began to set out the plates, bread, cheese, and cold meat for breakfast.

Essie entered, dressed in one of the sets of tunics and trousers, these ones in a deep green. As soon as her gaze landed on the table, she smiled, the expression lighting her face and sparkling in her eyes.

A smile twitched at his own mouth at the sight. "*Renatir.*"

Her forehead scrunched, telling him she did not recognize the word.

"That means *good morning* in elvish." Farrendel waited for her to take a seat before he sat across from her. This was only the third morning that they had eaten breakfast together, and only the second one here in the privacy of their rooms. It felt intimate, sharing a meal with her like this, and he wanted to treasure it.

Essie attempted to repeat the word, but it sounded nothing like it.

Farrendel tried to stuff his smile back as he repeated it again for her, slower.

She tried again, and if anything she butchered the word even worse.

He tried to hold back his grimace. He really did.

"That bad?" Essie winced and tried to say it a third time.

He could not help it. He full-on grimaced that time.

Essie snorted, then burst into laughter. "The look on your face…"

Strange how fast she could make his grimace turn into a smile. What was it about Essie that just made him want to smile?

Through her laughter, she said the word yet again, this time with a twinkle in her eyes.

He eyed her, trying to appear put out. "Now you are doing that on purpose."

"Maybe." She grinned, then pointed at her food. "What's the elvish word for this?"

Breakfast took a long time as he told her the elvish words for each of the parts of the food, for the plate, the fork, the chair, the table, and pretty much everything else she could point at while they ate.

When they finished, Farrendel washed the dishes while Essie dried them. As she dried her hands after the last dish, she turned to him. "What do you normally do all day? Yesterday I finished all my letters for my family and got those sent off. So I don't have anything else to do today."

Right. Farrendel winced and looked at the floor rather than Essie. He did not want to admit that he usually did very little each day. He practiced with his swords. He read. He went to court functions when he could not avoid it.

But other than that, he did not do much. He was too mentally weary between battles to force himself to accomplish anything.

"I read." Farrendel still could not bring himself to look at her. "We can see if we can find a book in Escarlish for you in the library."

"I looked when I wandered through there while you were gone, but the library is massive, and I didn't dare ask anyone for help." Essie shrugged, the movement visible at the corner of his eye. "Do you have elven stories translated into Escarlish? That doesn't seem like something you elves would bother with."

"I do not know." Farrendel peeked at her. By her posture, she did not seem too thrilled by the prospect. This was Essie. While he was happy hiding away doing nothing, Essie was likely going stir-crazy. "Perhaps...we could meet Illyna and some of the others to discuss your ideas about events to help wounded elf warriors. Perhaps tomorrow?"

He was not up for socializing today. But with a day to

prepare and get used to the thought of going out, he would be all right.

She smiled, straightening. "That sounds like a great plan. If we can't find anything I can read in the library, I can always start brainstorming ideas and organizing them before we discuss them with your friends."

He nodded. He was not sure how much he would be able to contribute, but she sounded so excited about her idea.

"In that case, let's sneak to the library." Essie grinned and held out her hand to him.

"Sneak?" Slowly, he reached out and clasped her first two fingers in the elven manner of holding hands.

"Yes, sneak. You don't sound too thrilled about seeing people." Her grin took on a mischievous tilt. "Besides, sneaking is more fun."

Sneaking was more fun. Especially with her.

Together, they stepped from his rooms. His branch was deserted, but the rest of Ellonahshinel would be bustling at this time of mid-morning. Not the best time for sneaking.

Not that they were truly sneaking from the servants. It was only his family they were truly trying to avoid, at least for now. And pretty much anyone from the elven court. They would sneer at Farrendel for being illegitimate—something he had yet to confess to Essie—and, worse, sneer at her for being human and marrying him.

Yes, sneaking was definitely the better option.

Holding Essie's hand, he took a winding path through Ellonahshinel to avoid going anywhere near Weylind's study or the parts of the treetop palace that were busiest at this time of day.

Occasionally, they passed a servant, and they ducked onto different branches or onto nearby porches.

As they neared the section where the library was located, the branches became more crowded with clerks, officials, and servants going about their duties in the quiet, dignified manner of the elves.

Farrendel ducked into the shelter of a leaf-covered branch, peering around it at the branch pathway that would take them to the library. When he spotted Weylind's clerk, he ducked back out of sight, holding his breath.

As he waited for the official to stroll by, he became aware of how close Essie was beside him, even if only the backs of their hands and their fingers were touching. With anyone else, he would have gotten an itching, crawling sensation at being so close to someone else. Even with his family, he sometimes got that feeling when they clasped his shoulders.

Yet with Essie, he had the urge to pull her closer. He would not. But the thought was there.

Once the official strolled by, Farrendel released a breath. His sigh must have been louder than he meant since, next to him, Essie giggled softly, pressing her free hand to her mouth.

He peeked out again, only to duck into hiding when he spotted Jalissa headed their way, on her way to the library.

Not good. While Jalissa had not been as hard on Essie as some of his other siblings, he did not want to run into her right now. He would see her at dinner that night with the rest of the family.

"Come on," he whispered as he urged Essie deeper into the concealing foliage.

That just had her stifling even more giggles.

Through the leaves, he could just make out Jalissa as she glided by on the branch. She glanced in their direction, though Farrendel held still. She would not be able to see them through the leaves and the shadows.

After a moment, she continued on, disappearing inside the library.

Essie let out a breath, giggling louder.

He eyed her. "Giggling is not conducive to sneaking."

Anyone else might have taken his baleful tone and blank expression for criticism or a demand to stop.

But Essie must have recognized the words for what they were—a joke—since she laughed and squeezed his fingers. "Yes, but it is rather funny. A prince of the elves sneaking around his own palace and hiding from his sister."

A hint of a smile twitched onto his face, as much of an answering laugh as he could manage. Somehow, Essie instinctively understood his dry sense of humor.

And even more amazing, he apparently still *had* a sense of humor.

It felt like a taste of being truly alive again.

He shook himself and forced himself to tiptoe forward. When he peeked through the leaves, the way to the library remained clear.

Tugging Essie with him, he hurried along the branch at something faster than a walk but not quite a run. They all but fell into the library, Essie laughing again, earning them a glare from the library attendant at the front desk.

But he did not care. How long had it been since he had smiled and simply had fun like he did with Essie?

He glanced around, but Jalissa had already disappeared deeper into the library. Good.

Farrendel pulled himself together and faced the attendant. "Do you have any elven primers or dictionaries that would aid in learning elvish?"

The attendant peered down his nose at Essie. "I suppose we still have the primers you used as a child."

Essie straightened, her giggles transforming to her princess smile. She did not need to understand the words to hear the disdain in the elf's voice.

The attendant motioned, and another elf—this one a female also dressed in the plain green of a servant in Ellonahshinel—appeared from around the shelves. The desk attendant explained what he wanted in a low tone, and she bustled off.

Farrendel waited, his fingers still clasping Essie's. She stayed silent as well.

Finally, the female servant returned, and she held out a stack of books to Farrendel. "Here are the books you requested, amir."

"Linshi." Farrendel had to let go of Essie's hand to take the stack of books with both hands. With a nod, he directed Essie back the way they had come.

As soon as they were on the porch surrounding the library, Essie released a breath and grinned. "Now we sneak back?"

"Yes." Farrendel led the way, though this time their trip was uneventful and less giggle-filled than before.

When they returned to their main room, Farrendel set the books on the table and sorted through them. There was an elvish-Escarlish dictionary, along with several basic primers designed to teach elven children how to read.

He paused on one book, recognizing it all too well.

"What's that?" Essie opened the book, her eyes

widening as she caught sight of the scribbles and doodles defacing the page. "I didn't realize elven children were just as naughty as human children when it came to scribbling in their school books."

"I did that. Most of it." Farrendel shifted, then pointed at a stick figure wielding what looked like a massive sword. "I wanted to be a warrior like my father and brother. Fighting sounded like more fun than learning to read."

How naïve he had been, as a child. He had seen battles as places of adventure and glory, not the place of death and blood as he now knew. Later, as he had gotten older, he had switched to wanting to be a healer.

And then he had gotten his deadly magic, and he had become a warrior after all.

Essie's expression turned solemn, and she rested her hand over his on the page. "These drawings are still cute. Even if you now see how innocent you were compared to what you know now."

He drew in a deep breath and forced the melancholy away. He wanted to go back to the laughter and fun of moments ago.

Farrendel forced a twitch to his mouth as he shut the book and held it out to her. "Would you like to begin?"

Essie took the book and headed for the mounds of cushions on the far side of the room. "Sure. I need to learn to speak elvish as soon as possible. I can recognize a few spoken words, though I can understand more in writing. But it would be nice not to be so lost whenever everyone else is speaking."

She might not like being able to understand the elvish spoken, especially if his fellow elves continued to make snide comments to her face even after she could understand them.

But she deserved to be able to understand what was being said around her.

Farrendel sat on one of the cushions facing her. He was not exactly qualified for teaching someone a new language, but who else were they going to ask?

No, they would just have to muddle through it as best they could. Besides, it was something to do with her, at least. And more than anything, he found that he enjoyed spending time with her.

THIS TIME when Farrendel clasped Essie's fingers as he strolled the back streets of Estyra, it did not feel so odd or new. Instead, he had the strange urge to pull her even closer, despite the fact that they were in public. He had never felt anything like this before. Ever.

As they neared the café near Illyna's shop, his stomach flipped with renewed nerves. He was not even sure why he was so nervous. He knew Fingol and Fydella would like Essie. Just about everyone—besides his family, it seemed—liked Essie. Essie would like Fingol and Fydella. She liked everyone and managed to be gracious even to those who snubbed her.

Yet he was still nervous. He could not help it.

As they approached Farrendel's usual table in a sheltered corner in the back, Fingol and Fydella stood, bobbing small bows.

Farrendel drew in a deep breath, trying to force himself to calm. "Essie, this is Fingol and his wife Fydella. Fingol, Fydella, this is my wife, Essie. Princess Elspeth."

"It is a pleasure to meet you, amirah." Fydella smiled with genuine warmth. If only Farrendel's family had greeted Essie with the same warmth.

"It's a pleasure to meet both of you as well." Essie slid into the seat with her back to the rest of the café, leaving the chair with its back to the tree for Farrendel. "Farrendel has mentioned both of you many times."

He had? Farrendel took his seat, thankful that Essie had known enough to choose the other one. They had talked a lot about his friends in the past few days as Essie planned her ideas for fundraising events to help the wounded elven warriors, but he had not realized she had paid such close attention.

An elf glided up to their table. Farrendel ordered his usual while Fingol and Fydella also ordered. Essie glanced at the paper menu, her smile dipping for a moment, before she pointed at the menu as if at random. "I'll have this."

The server blinked, then her gaze dropped to where Essie's finger was pointed. The server nodded, made a note on a paper, and left.

As they waited for their food, Essie asked Fingol about what he did, and Farrendel mostly listened as Fingol talked about his business carving items out of wood. He had some plant growing magic, but it was not strong. He used it to enhance his natural skill, but much of his carving was done by hand rather than magic.

The server returned and set their food in front of them.

Farrendel watched Essie's face, searching for any sign that she was disappointed with what she had ordered.

Essie glanced over her plate, then smiled. "This looks delicious."

He relaxed. He had not wanted to switch with her, but he would have if he had to.

She glanced at his plate. "Yours looks good as well. I'll have to taste a bite. If you don't mind."

Taste a bite? As in, eat some of his? But this meal was his. He could not wrap his mind around the thought of sharing food like that.

Yet he managed a nod. He did not want to tell her no. It must be some kind of human custom.

Essie, Fydella, and Fingol kept up a steady conversation. Farrendel participated occasionally, but it was relaxing to just listen to them.

Partway through, Essie reached over to his plate, her fork hovering just over a section of his food. She glanced at him, as if asking his permission.

She wanted her taste. Farrendel sliced off a corner and nudged it to the edge of his plate.

Her smile flashed across her face before she speared the bite he had set aside for her. When she ate the bite, she nodded. "That is good too."

When they finished their meal and the server collected their plates, Essie outlined her ideas. "In Escarland, a princess's duty often involves working with charities, especially when it comes to fundraising. We use our position of power and prestige to draw attention to causes. I'm not saying that I'm coming in here as a stranger trying to rescue any of you. I would like to bring some of my Escarlish ideas to the table, as it were. If there is anything I can do to help with organization or planning, I would like to do so. All I want to do is offer my help. You are the ones who know best what you need and what should be done to truly help those elves wounded in the war, especially those permanently injured."

Fingol nodded, then glanced at Farrendel, meeting his gaze for a moment before turning back to Essie. "It is a good idea to start a more formal network so that we can help each other. We already do it, but it is an unofficial thing. But the two of you are in a unique position to do that. Our Laesornysh is well beloved among those who have fought at his side. We have banded together out of our loyalty to him."

Farrendel shifted, his gaze dropping to his hands. He did not deserve their loyalty. Yes, he fought and fought hard to protect Tarenhiel and its warriors. But all he had truly done was get himself captured and have to be rescued, leading to many deaths, including the death of his dacha.

Fydella nodded. "Illyna has been doing much of the organization that we already have in place."

"I figured as much." Essie nodded. "Of course we'll want to bring her on board and see if she's willing to help with this."

"I am sure she will be." Fingol reached down and rubbed his bad leg, though Farrendel doubted he realized he was doing it. "She has mentioned something like this before, but we've had no one volunteer to spend the time to actually put it together."

"Time is something I have plenty of right now." Essie shrugged.

Farrendel winced. He would have to tell her soon that he and Weylind had a planned tour of duty at the border coming up. He would be gone for three weeks or more.

At least she would have this project to work on. And she now knew Illyna, Fingol, and Fydella better than she had when he had left last time.

Still, he was not ready to leave her again. He would

much rather stay here and continue teaching her elvish and watching the excitement in her eyes as she came up with ideas and plans.

But he would not shirk his duty. He had to protect his kingdom. All he could hope was that this tour was quiet and free from any raids.

FOURTEEN

F arrendel set his pack on the ground by the door before he faced Essie. Outside the windows, darkness had fully fallen. He and Weylind would travel through the night to reach the border by morning.

They planned to be gone for three weeks, joining the patrols and fending off any troll raids. Assuming the trolls did not launch any major offensives. If that happened, they would stay at the border until the trolls were turned back.

Now all that was left to do was say goodbye to Essie. He had already said goodbye to his family at supper. Those goodbyes were almost routine at this point. Yes, they were all aware that he or Weylind might never return. Yet they had said these goodbyes many times over.

Saying this kind of goodbye with Essie was new. Last time had been an unplanned rush to the border to turn back a raid. This time, the leave-taking was planned. Last time, they had only been married a few days. Now, he had gotten to know her better. Something was happening between them. Something he could not name or fully understand. But it made this goodbye feel...important.

Essie faced him, a forced smile on her face. "I guess this is farewell until you return."

He nodded. He should say something. Anything. He could not just turn and walk away like he had last time. She deserved so much better than that. But he could not seem to get the words put together inside his head, much less force them out of his mouth.

"I'll be all right. I'll be so busy working with Illyna, Fydella, and Fingol on our plans and learning elvish that I won't even notice you're gone." She gave a wavering smile, to show that it was more a joke to make him feel better.

He gave another nod, still struggling to come up with words. It did make him feel better, knowing that she would not be left as alone as she had been last time. Especially since he would be gone far longer.

Essie shifted, her gaze searching his face. "Would you write to me? Or at least send a message or two along your elven root system? Just to let me know you're all right? I can write you back, if letters will reach you."

"I would like that." Something inside his chest eased at the thought of receiving her words while at the border. It would not be as nice as being with her but hearing her voice in the words would be a light he had never had before while fighting at the border. "I will write."

"Thanks." Essie remained where she was, as if even she did not know what to do or say.

Farrendel opened his bag and pulled his seal out of a side pocket. He held it out to her. "Here. Use my seal.

Your letters to your family or to me should not be tampered with under your seal but..."

"But I am a foreign princess. Your people are still understandably suspicious." Essie took the seal from him, and her fingers brushed against his, sending his heart rate beating harder at her soft touch.

He cleared his throat and nodded. He had been personally handing her letters to the messengers to make sure they were delivered without being read. But for the next three weeks, he would not be here. This was the best protection he could give her.

Hopefully it would be enough. He had yet to tell her that he was illegitimate, something that would make his seal mean less than it should. Yet he was still a prince, even an illegitimate one. Few would dare open his seal, especially since they would know Weylind would back Farrendel if it came to that.

He closed his pack again as the silence lengthened. He did not want to leave, even though the train was already waiting at the station.

When he straightened, he found that Essie had stepped a little bit closer, his seal still clutched in her hand. "Would you mind if I hugged you farewell?"

He froze. She had hugged him before, once. It had been unexpectedly pleasant. More, it was something that he found himself longing to experience again.

Perhaps that was why his head tilted in a nod even before he had truly thought it through.

Essie moved slowly enough that he could have pulled away, if he had wished. Her arms came around him, and she embraced him, resting her head against his shoulder.

His breath caught, and he was not sure what to do with his arms. She was warm and soft against him, and he found himself wanting to draw her closer. If he dared.

Slowly, he wrapped one arm around her and rested his hand on her back.

If anything, she snuggled closer. As if she liked him embracing her.

He liked holding her. He had never realized how it would feel. Normally, he did not like having people close. But Essie was different. And what he felt when he was with her was different.

After a long moment, she pulled back. "Stay safe."

Before he could think of any reply, she stood on her tiptoes and kissed his cheek, her lips soft as they brushed his skin.

Was he still breathing? His brain was fizzling. Blindly, Farrendel fumbled for his pack, turned, and stumbled out the door. He did not even remember walking the pathways of Ellonahshinel until he met Weylind at the top of the stairs to the forest floor.

Weylind raised a questioning eyebrow, but Farrendel ignored him.

Somehow, Farrendel walked to the train station without any conscious thought. He barely noticed the people bustling along the streets, nor did he pay much attention to the sneering expression of Thanfardil, the elf in charge of arranging the train schedules, when the elf bowed to Weylind and assured him the tracks were cleared to the north.

Finally, Farrendel sank onto the bench in the seating car.

Essie had *kissed* him. On the cheek. But still. It had been a kiss.

And once again, he had neglected to tell her farewell.

What did she think of him? She had kissed him, and he had run.

At least he had managed to hug her back. It was a start.

He sighed and flopped back against the seat. And now he had three weeks or more to obsess over all the things he could have done better in that goodbye.

Weylind sat on the bench across from him, his dark eyes searching Farrendel's face. "Is something wrong, shashon?"

"I am fine." Farrendel was not about to talk about any of this with his brother.

Weylind scowled, the lines around his mouth deepening. "Did *she* do or say something?"

"No." Yes. But not anything bad, the way Weylind meant it. "I do not want to talk about it."

Farrendel pushed to his feet, brushed past Weylind, and retreated to his private train car.

He sprawled on the bed, staring at the broad windows as the night-shadowed trees flashed by. Perhaps, if he thought about Essie and that kiss on his cheek instead of the border and the war that lay ahead, he might even get some sleep.

DRESSED IN HIS FIGHTING LEATHERS, Farrendel perched on a branch high in a tree, taking a quiet moment as the sun rose a week after he had arrived at the border. So far, this patrol had been quiet. Farrendel and Weylind had traveled between the camps along the border, spending a few days at each.

As of yet, there had been no troll raids across the

border. Nor had the scouts sent across the border reported any movements by the troll army. So far, the only unusual thing they had reported were the tracks left by several small bands of trolls that appeared to dart into Tarenhiel during the night before returning, yet their purpose remained a mystery. They did not raid any towns and appeared to do their best to avoid the elven warriors.

From his perch, Farrendel could just make out the edge of the Gulmorth Gorge. A cold breeze shivered down from the Kostarian mountains, tossing his hair. The layers of his leathers kept him plenty warm while his swords were a reassuring weight against his back.

After glancing around to ensure that he was still alone, Farrendel pulled out Essie's recent letter. The folds were already worn because he had read and re-read it so many times.

Unfolding it, he read the letter again, letting the words soak into him. If he closed his eyes, he could almost hear Essie's voice echoing in her writing.

She was staying busy, planning an event with Illyna and Fydella. She had also had tea with Machasheni Leyleira again, which she claimed had been pleasant. To close the letter, she attempted a line in elvish. Some of her grammar was not perfect, but he could understand the sentence.

Between the quiet and Essie's letters, the darkness did not seem as bad along the border as it usually did.

With her words still calming his muscles, he carefully folded the letter and tucked it into an inner pocket near his heart. Yes, it was the gesture of a hopeless romantic. But he liked the feel of having her close. Perhaps he would even get up the courage to tell her just that when he returned home to her.

A clear note blared into the morning air.

He stilled, his muscles tensing, his heart beating. An alarm horn.

Farrendel leapt from his perch, landing lightly on the mossy ground. He raced toward the camp. As he neared, he could already hear Weylind and the commanders calling orders. Farrendel halted next to Weylind.

Weylind's face was hard. "The scouts have reported a raid to the east."

He did not have to explain further. Their patrol would muster and attempt to cut the raid off from the gorge.

In minutes, the commanders were leading squads of warriors into the forest. Farrendel fell into step at Weylind's side as they ghosted through the forest at the head of their own squads of warriors.

Long minutes stretched as they jogged silently until the crashing and clanging from ahead echoed from the rocks of the Gulmorth Gorge and the stately trees on this side of the border.

Weylind motioned that he would lead the others forward while Farrendel circled around to get between the gorge and the trolls. The other patrols were circling around to come at the raiders from the other side.

After one last shared glance with Weylind, Farrendel drew his swords, ice flooding through his veins as he prepared to go into battle. He stuck to the trees and foliage, staying hidden as he crept around the sounds of fighting coming from the woods ahead of him.

He dropped behind a large boulder, his back sheltered by another rock. Ahead of him, a line of troll warriors charged the elven warriors.

With the blast of the elven horn, Weylind led the charge from the forest. His black hair whipped around him as he wielded his single sword. Roots and branches lashed out around him as he whirled into battle, reminding everyone that the elven king was a great warrior in his own right.

The troll warriors faltered, then took a step back as if they intended to retreat.

Farrendel stood and let his magic flow from him. It crackled down his arms and the length of his swords. "Surrender."

The faltering trolls formed a circle, their jaws hardening and eyes flashing.

Farrendel resisted the urge to sigh as he hardened his own resolve. The trolls would not surrender, despite the fact that they were surrounded and outnumbered. They considered it more honorable to die in battle than to surrender to an elf.

With Weylind and the elven warriors so close, Farrendel could not unleash his magic beyond the tightly controlled crackling coating his swords. Instead, he leapt off the boulder and launched himself at the trolls, stabbing down with his swords. He kicked a troll sword out of the way as he came down.

Reinforced with his magic, his swords sliced through metal and bone easily. He could not let himself think about the blood. The slaughter. The death. Until the ground was littered with bodies and his swords were coated with blood.

Farrendel rested a shaking hand over the place where Essie's letter remained safely tucked inside his fighting leathers. The light and joy of her words were a distant memory in this place of war and death.

Weylind halted next to him and rested a hand on his shoulder. He did not say anything. He did not have to.

His face was just as grim and hard as Farrendel's in the wake of so much death.

Farrendel forced away the shaking and, instead, swept a calculating glance over the battlefield. "This is small, for a raid."

Weylind nodded, the thoughtful lines returning around his mouth. "I am not sure what their purpose was in attacking here. There are no villages nearby."

"Perhaps they wished to catch one of our small patrols." Farrendel grimaced and tried not to feel the blood covering his fingers. All he wanted to do was scrub himself under scalding water until he felt clean again. "It was just their misfortune that our reinforcing patrol happened to be in the area."

"Maybe." Weylind's frown remained, as if he found that explanation plausible yet still sensed something off.

It did seem odd. Something had changed recently in the troll tactics, and that was never a good thing. What did it mean? What were the trolls planning?

And what would it mean for Farrendel, as the one who would be called upon to stop the trolls?

FARRENDEL TRUDGED along the branches of Ellonahshinel, his pack heavy against his back. At this time of night, only a few elven lights remained lit among the leaves, illuminating the branches in a soft glow.

Ahead, Weylind strolled along the branches. At the turnoff to his room, Weylind turned, his eyes studying Farrendel. He opened his mouth, probably for another lecture about Essie. Or his usual hovering.

Farrendel brushed past him. "I will be fine."

"Shashon..." Weylind reached to clasp Farrendel's shoulder, but Farrendel dodged around him.

"I am fine." Farrendel turned his back to Weylind and stalked along the branch toward his and Essie's rooms as quickly as possible. His back itched with the feel of Weylind's eyes watching him leave, but he did not turn around or slow. And, thankfully, Weylind did not attempt to follow.

Crickets and tree frogs sang softly into the night, but other than that, the evening remained quiet. So very peaceful after all the fighting.

Essie was likely already asleep. He should not feel disappointed that she would not be there when he returned. Yes, Weylind had sent a message that they would be returning tonight. But there was no reason Essie would stay up for Farrendel.

And yet, as Farrendel tiptoed across the final branch to their rooms, the lights of the main room were on, casting a bright glow into Ellonahshinel. Perhaps Essie had simply left the lights on for him so he would not return in the dark.

He eased the door open and crept inside, closing the door with a soft click behind him.

A noise came from behind him, and he whirled, his hand going to the hilt of his sword.

Essie was curled on the piles of cushions on the other side of the room, a blanket wrapped around her. Her red hair frizzed from its braid while her expression held the sleepy befuddlement of someone woken from a deep sleep. She stretched and yawned. "You're back!"

He let his pack fall to the floor, frozen where he stood.

She had waited up for him. Not only that, but she

looked so adorable all sleepy and befuddled that it twisted something inside him.

"I must have fallen asleep while I was waiting." Essie pushed to her feet, clutching the blanket around her shoulders, and padded across the room until she stood in front of him. "Welcome back."

Then, she held out her arms, offering a hug even though she did not force one on him. She just waited, letting him decide if he wanted one or not.

Something broke inside him. He stepped forward and found himself wrapping his arms around her before he had thought it through. Yet as he pulled her close, it felt so *right* that he did not pull away.

Essie tightened her arms around him, snuggling closer. "I'm so glad you're back safe and sound. And thanks for your letters. I really appreciated hearing that you were all right."

His letters had not been long or detailed. But he had made an effort. It was the least he could do when she had written several letters a week the entire time he had been gone. He had received so many that he had not been able to keep all of them in his inner pocket since they would not fit.

He rested his cheek against her hair, still holding her close. "I liked your letters. I kept them in my pocket. Over my heart."

Now the tips of his ears were burning. At least Essie could not tell with her face pressed against his shoulder. Why had he said that out loud?

Her arms squeezed him tighter. "I'm glad they helped. I was afraid they were rather rambling."

"They made me smile." He had not thought anything could do that while he was patrolling the border.

"Good." Essie gave him one last squeeze before she stepped back, though she stayed close enough that his hands still rested on her waist, and it seemed so natural that he did not let her go. She rested a hand on his chest, drawing his attention to her face. "You'll probably have nightmares tonight, won't you? Is there any point in going to bed, or should I just wait down here since I'll be coming back down in an hour or two?"

She already knew him too well. And it hurt something inside him that *this* was something she needed to know to be a part of his life.

He sighed and could not bring himself to meet her gaze. "You should get some sleep tonight. Do not get up on my account. Tonight will not be the only one with nightmares."

The darkness crowded into the edges of his vision at the thought of facing the upcoming nightmares. The next few days would be a blur of nightmares and fatigue. It would be a week or more before he began to crawl his way out and feel like a person again.

"Ah." Essie's hand shifted on his chest, dragging his attention away from the darkness and back to her. Her smile remained soft as she reached up and touched his cheek. "All right. I'll try to get some sleep tonight. But I'll meet you down here tomorrow night and every night after that until the nightmares aren't as bad, all right?"

He nodded, unable to process both words and her touch on his cheek at the same time.

She stepped all the way back. "In that case, we probably should both head for bed, if we're going to get any sleep tonight."

Farrendel blindly fumbled for his bag and snagged it from where it had dropped on the floor. By the time he straightened, Essie had crossed the room and had her hand on her door.

She turned back to him, giving him another smile. "Goodnight. I hope you sleep well."

He hoped so too. For her sake, as much as his own.

As she opened her door, he drew in a deep breath. He could not let her just walk away as he had so many times before. "Essie…"

She glanced around the door frame at him. "Yes?"

He opened his mouth, but the word stuck in his throat. This should not be this hard. It was one word. Not even something personal. He closed his mouth, swallowed, and tried again. "Goodnight."

Her smile widened into that beaming one that sparkled in her eyes and warmed him all the way to the depths of his heart.

CHAPTER

FIFTEEN

Another patrol along the border. More battle and blood. Another late night return.

And now, another round of nightmares keeping him awake in the middle of the night.

He stumbled down the stairs to the main room and sank onto the piles of cushions. Essie was not there yet. Perhaps she had managed to sleep through his screams this time? It would be best if she had. They had that event for wounded elven warriors tomorrow that she had been planning for months. She should be well rested, even if he was not.

But no. Scuffling footsteps sounded on the stairs a moment before the door opened and Essie tottered into the room, rubbing her eyes. Yawning, she slumped onto the cushions next to him. "I had hoped we would get a good night's sleep tonight, at least. I guess that was probably too much to hope for."

"I am sorry." Perhaps he should have stayed at the

border a few more days instead of hurrying back in time for the event. Then she would have gotten plenty of sleep.

"I'd gladly give up sleep to have you here." Essie sent him a sleepy smile as she sagged against the wall behind her. "I'm glad you made it back in time. They're coming because of you, not me. You are their Laesornysh. Their hero and wounded prince."

Farrendel resisted the urge to squirm as he stared into the darkness of the main room. Only the faintest hint of starlight filtered through the dense foliage of Ellon-ahshinel.

Did his fellow elf warriors see him that way? As a leader among them? Sure, he used the wealth he had as a prince to frequent places owned by wounded warriors like Illyna and Fingol. Many had become his friends.

But he had never done anything to earn their loyalty. Not really.

It was humbling to know that he had it anyway.

"Now, I think it was my turn to tell an Escarlish tale." Essie grinned as she squirmed into what was probably a more comfortable position.

Over the past months of nightmares, he and Essie had taken to telling Tarenhieli and Escarlish folktales to pass the time during the long nights after his nightmares. So far, he had avoided telling her the tale of Daesyn and Inara. He was not yet ready to explain about the elishina, nor did he want Essie to think he was pressuring her into anything. Right now, he liked the way their relationship was forming in its own time and way.

Essie had not asked for the tale of Daesyn and Inara either, even though Machasheni Leyleira had mentioned it at their wedding. Perhaps she, too, was not yet ready to push for anything more.

Farrendel closed his eyes and settled onto the cushions as Essie started the tale. As she talked, he shifted until he was lying down, his muscles relaxing as the soothing sound of Essie's voice banished the nightmares back to the darkness where they belonged.

As she finished the tale with its requisite happy ending that all her tales seemed to possess, Farrendel cracked an eye open and peered at her. "Why did the prince have to use the shoe to find her?"

"They were masquerade balls. He never saw her face." Essie said it like it was obvious.

"But he saw her hair and heard her voice. He should have been able to recognize her even without the shoe." Farrendel worked to keep his voice bewildered rather than show his amusement. "Besides, he had only known her three nights. That was not nearly enough time to decide he wanted to marry her."

"You decided to marry me after only a few minutes." Essie smirked down at him.

She had a point. He probably should not critique the prince in the tale too much. "There were extenuating circumstances. We were trying to save our kingdoms."

"And she was trying to escape her abusive home life while he was trying to escape an arranged marriage. I'd say those were extenuating circumstances as well."

Hmm. He would have to try harder if he was going to get her adorably frustrated. "What do you have against an arranged marriage?"

Instead of frustration, Essie tilted her head back to laugh. "I walked into that one, didn't I? Nothing, if it's an arranged marriage between the right people and the right kingdoms." The smile she sent him held the assurance that she thought theirs fit that category. "But not every arranged marriage is like that. Some are worth fleeing. And you have to admit, he was right, since it turned out the princess he was supposed to marry planned to murder him eventually."

Exactly Weylind's fear for Farrendel going into this arranged marriage. Perhaps human tales like this one had planted the idea in his brother's head?

Farrendel squirmed to get into a more comfortable position on his pile of cushions. Essie's smile and laughter was all well and good, but he would have to press this fake argument a little further if he wanted to annoy her. "And another thing. How did that pumpkin turn into a carriage? Magic does not work that way. It cannot transform one thing into another."

Essie huffed and rolled her eyes. "It's a story. Magic doesn't have to work the same way in stories as it does in real life."

There was the cute, annoyed look he had been going for. He fought to keep his smile from breaking through his blank expression. "It still is not very logical."

"In your last story, the elven maid's grief was so great that her tears watered the blood of her murdered lover, and the drops of his blood sprang into beautiful red flowers. That is not very logical either. Not to mention rather macabre. Don't you elves have any happy stories?"

They had the tale of Daesyn and Inara, but he was not ready to tell her that one just yet.

"We elves appreciate the beauty in grief." Farrendel kept his tone light. This conversation had banished the darkness, and he did not want it to take a turn in that direction.

"More like elves love the melodramatic." Essie

reached out and patted his shoulder. He was not even sure she was aware she had done it.

It was a sign of how comfortable she was becoming with him, that she would touch him without a thought.

And how comfortable he was becoming with her, that he would not flinch away when she did.

Essie kept right on talking, her hand leaving his shoulder to gesture at his hair. "Face it. You elves are all about style and flair. Who else would go into battle with long hair majestically flying on the breeze?"

"Our long hair serves a purpose." Now he was the one to take on that disgruntled tone. His hair helped him sense what was around him, especially while he was flipping in the air.

But he had the feeling it was a conversation that was going to be hard to explain to Essie. He did not think human hair had quite the same properties as elven hair.

"Uh-huh." Essie grinned and shrugged. "Even so, admit it. You elves aren't blind to the aesthetic."

He could not help but smile at that. She had a point there.

Perhaps, someday, he would explain the meaning given to an elf warrior's long hair and the dishonor of cutting it. And, sure, the aesthetic probably played a role in how long hair was considered honorable. Elves loved their ideal of perfect beauty, after all.

But that was a more serious topic than he wanted to broach right now.

Farrendel pushed into a sitting position. "You should return to bed and get some sleep."

Essie's eyes searched his face, though he was not sure how much she could see in the shadows. "Will you be able to sleep now?"

"I think so." At least, he hoped so. As long as his nightmares remained mild enough that he did not scream, he would not wake her. She would get some sleep, even if his sleep was restless.

"All right." Essie stood and headed for her door. As she opened it, she glanced over her shoulder. "Goodnight."

"Goodnight." He waited for her to leave before he pushed to his feet. Now to attempt a few hours of sleep. Tomorrow was going to be hard enough without trying to get through on little sleep.

FARRENDEL DREW in a deep breath through the tightness in his throat at being surrounded by so many people. Normally, he would not attend such a large gathering only a day after returning from yet another tour at the border.

But this was the event Essie had been planning for months. He had to be here, for her sake.

Besides, this was not the elven court with their sneering nobles peering down their noses at their illegitimate, scarred prince. These were his fellow warriors, bearing their own scars and burdens. Instead of sneering at him, they looked at him as their Laesornysh, their hero. And that adoration was nearly as uncomfortable as the sneers, though in a different way.

Though, his shoulder blades itched with the feeling of eyes on him. Farrendel swept a glance over the gathering —the clusters of elves talking, the groups around the refreshment tables, the tables for business owners and elves looking for jobs to gather—but he could not see anyone out of place.

Many of the elves here had a visible scar, missing limb, or other permanent injury. Several elves leaned on canes. Others had wooden hands that they moved using their growing magic. Still others had scars that were far less visible but no less real.

It was good to see them all gathered together, smiling, laughing, and talking. Farrendel hoped this night worked as Essie had intended and brought together those searching for jobs with those who were hiring.

Essie stood a few feet away, attempting to make use of her newfound elvish skills. The elf she was talking to had scrunched eyebrows and an uncomprehending expression.

Farrendel stepped to Essie's side. Time to translate. She was getting better, especially when it came to understanding spoken elvish. But her Escarlish accent was thick for anyone who was not used to it.

She glanced at him and asked in Escarlish, "What did I say wrong?"

"Your Escarlish accent is thick." He could feel a smile twitching the corners of his mouth.

She sighed with resignation. "How is it supposed to sound?"

He said the greeting, and she repeated it several times until she had it right. By that time, Farrendel was struggling to hold back his smile, and the other elf was quietly laughing.

This was what Essie brought all of them. Laughter. Hope.

And she showed Farrendel how he could be helping his fellow warriors more. He might be the illegitimate prince, but he still had power and resources. He could approach Weylind with any changes or laws that were necessary. He had access to the elven court, even if he was an outcast among them.

He was not sure what he could do or how he should do it. But Essie would know, and she would help him.

If only they could end the war with the trolls. That would be the best thing they could do, even if it was a distant dream at this point.

ANOTHER NIGHT. Another nightmare.

Farrendel leaned against the wall in the main room, his throat still aching from his screams and his eyes aching after so many sleepless nights in a row.

Essie curled up on the cushions next to him, so close that their arms were brushing. But she did not pull away, and he did not either.

After a moment, Essie yawned, eased even closer, and leaned her head against his shoulder.

Farrendel's breath caught in his chest. But he managed not to flinch away from her. No, this was actually…nice. Better than nice.

Her head was a heavy weight on his shoulder as she slumped even more against him. "I'll try to stay awake if you want me to…" Her words ended in another yawn.

"Rest." Farrendel took her hand, then shifted so that her head rested more comfortably against him. After staying up late telling him the folktale the night before, then the busy day at the event, Essie needed her rest. Besides, he had not had a chance to come up with a new elven tale to tell her. He leaned his head on top of hers. "Linshi."

"No problem," Essie mumbled as she drifted back to sleep. Only moments later, her breathing evened and her body relaxed with sleep.

Farrendel held her close, his muscles relaxing after the tension of the nightmare.

In another month, they would leave for Lethorel, and he would finally have a chance to truly rest. Maybe, in that rest, he could finally process these thoughts and feelings he had when he was with Essie.

He liked her. A lot. He liked how she had thrown herself into helping the wounded warriors with such a passion, simply because she had gotten to know him and his struggles. He liked how she was genuinely kind to everyone, even his family who seemed determined to not like her. She was so caring and giving and bubbly and just...Essie.

He had never felt like this about anyone. And that would take a bit of processing to get it settled inside his muddled mind and heart.

But Essie was worth it.

SIXTEEN

F arrendel waited off to the side with Essie while
his family said farewell to Melantha and
Leyleira, the only two who were not going to
Lethorel with them.

"Are you sure you do not want to come, isciena?"
Weylind gripped Melantha's shoulders. "Machasheni is
capable of looking after the kingdom while we are gone."

"Of course I am." Machasheni released Rheva from a
shoulder-grip hug and eyed Melantha. "You should go
and enjoy time with your family."

Melantha shook her head, a strange look in her eyes.
"No, I am fine. I prefer to remain here this year."

Beside Farrendel, Essie tensed. Was Melantha
remaining behind because of Essie? Farrendel hoped not.
He had thought his family had at least gotten to a point
where they could tolerate Essie. It was far from the
wholehearted embracing her as family that he would
prefer, especially since he was well on his way to falling
for her, but he would take any progress that he could get.

After giving Melantha another sharp look that had her squirming, Machasheni turned to Jalissa, speaking quietly.

Melantha stepped back, her gaze darting to where Farrendel and Essie stood. That strange look crossed her face again, and her expression twisted for just a moment before she looked away.

Farrendel suppressed a sigh. Apparently Melantha was not even going to take the time to say farewell to him because of Essie.

He was not sure what was going on with Melantha. She had been upset when he and Weylind had returned from the diplomatic meeting with a signed treaty and Essie in tow, and she had only become more withdrawn since then.

Perhaps some time with just her and Machasheni Leyleira here at Estyra was just what Melantha would need. If anyone could get at the heart of what was going on with Melantha, it was Machasheni.

After finishing with Jalissa, Machasheni strode to Essie and Farrendel. A hint of a smile played on her face. "I trust the two of you will enjoy your stay at Lethorel."

"I'm sure we will." Essie glanced up at him. "Farrendel hasn't stopped talking about it for weeks now."

Had he? He supposed he had talked about it more than he had anything else in the past few weeks. He always looked forward to the rest found at Lethorel, but he was especially excited to show the place to Essie.

"I am sure he has." Machasheni's smile turned a little extra knowing as she swung her gaze to Farrendel. "Make the most of your time at Lethorel, sasonsheni."

What did she mean by that? Before Farrendel had a

chance to even think about a response, Machasheni swept off, headed back toward Ellonahshinel.

Weylind, Rheva, Brina, Ryfon, and Jalissa were boarding the train, and Essie turned to join them.

Out of the corner of his eye, Farrendel caught sight of Melantha talking to Thanfardil, the elf in charge of all the train schedules in Tarenhiel. They were talking so low that Farrendel could not hear anything of what they were saying.

Strange, but Farrendel shrugged it away and followed Essie toward the train.

On board, he settled onto the cushioned bench in the seating car, taking the seat next to Essie. Within minutes, the train eased into motion.

Finally, they were on their way to Lethorel. Unless something major happened, there would be no war, no blood, no battles for the next three weeks.

FARRENDEL COULD NOT HELP the twitch of a smile as Essie bounced in her seat and craned her neck to see as much of the passing forest through the train's broad, curving windows as she possibly could, even though hours had passed since they had boarded the train in Estyra.

On his other side, Ryfon and Brina sat reservedly, though their gazes strayed from Essie to the windows as if they were tempted to act just as excited if they had been raised with less elven dignity.

Across the way, Jalissa, Weylind, and Rheva rested sedately on the cushioned bench. Both Rheva and Weylind were reading through paperwork while Jalissa stared silently out the windows, her hands folded serenely in her lap.

Next to Farrendel, Essie all but smushed her face against the window. "How long until we get there?"

Farrendel found himself full-on smiling. "We will arrive in Arorien, a small town, this evening. Then we will ride to Lethorel by horseback the next morning."

He straightened, his stomach tightening. Could Essie ride? He had never thought to ask. While elves had trains, they were still a relatively new invention, and elves still rode many places.

But the humans had used trains for as long as Essie had been alive. And he had gotten the impression that human royalty took carriages most places, rather than ride.

He turned toward Essie. "Can you ride? I did not think to ask."

Thankfully, Essie grinned and plopped onto her seat so that she was facing the others rather than the windows. "Yes, of course, I ride. It is one of the skills considered proper for a lady of the Escarlish court. I also know archery. It was all the rage for the court ladies a few years ago."

For the first time that trip, Jalissa straightened and faced Essie, interest brightening her expression. "Are you any good?"

Essie shrugged, a wry tilt to her mouth. "I was all right. I'm better with a rifle, but I'm assuming you probably don't have any here. I'd love to brush up on my archery, even if my skills can't compare with your elf archers."

Jalissa's smile warmed, as if she was glad to find something in common with her human sister-in-law. "We will have to test that. I love archery, and there are several spare bows at Lethorel. I believe Farrendel's old bow is still there."

Ah, yes. He had spent hours of boredom attempting to improve his archery skills. Only to realize, in the end, that archery simply was not his thing. But it had helped pass the long days when it had been just Dacha, Farrendel, and Jalissa at Lethorel while Farrendel had been growing up. "I was never any good. I always preferred my swords. Besides, it is not really my bow. I just was the last to have it handed down to me."

"It sounds like a lot of fun." Essie's grin widened further, and she inched a little closer to him. "This place sounds really special to all of you. I gathered that when we talked about it at dinner, but all of you are happier the closer we get."

How much did he dare tell her? He had yet to tell her that he was illegitimate, the reason he had spent much of his childhood isolated at Lethorel to protect him from the sneering pettiness of the court. "I spent much of my childhood there."

Strangely, Essie did not ask why, though that could have been because she did not want to ask prying questions while his family was staring at them. She knew how opening up in front of others made him uncomfortable.

Instead, she smiled brightly, as if to dissipate the heaviness that had descended on the train car at the reference to a tense time in their family. "My family has a similar summer cottage. My mother would take us there as often as she could when we were growing up. It is hard growing up under the scrutiny of the court all the time. At that cottage, we had a chance to be children. I imagine Lethorel must be like that for you, though you weren't all children at the same time the way me and my brothers were. One of the few memories I have of my father is at that cottage."

Farrendel stared at the floor, unable to look at Essie or at his family. "Yes, Lethorel is like that for us."

"Father was able to love all of us best at Lethorel. Some of my best memories of us as a family are there." Jalissa's voice was quiet, breaking just a bit.

Farrendel did not lift his gaze, but he could hear the faint creaking of the cushions as Weylind shifted.

No one spoke, but there was a wealth of memories in the silence. At Lethorel, their family had been just a little less broken. Dacha had smiled again—laughed again—while there.

And yet, it had also reinforced just how shattered the family was. Weylind, Melantha, and Jalissa had memories there with their macha. Dacha had retreated there, choosing to protect Farrendel instead of spending time with the others in Estyra. Farrendel had spent most of his childhood there, happy and yet rather lonely much of the time.

He turned toward the window, fighting the urge to retreat. His private train car was hitched to this train— Weylind knew better than to leave it behind in case Farrendel needed space—even if they would be spending the night in Arorien instead of on the train. A show of supporting the townsfolk rather than keeping to themselves like stuffy royalty.

Before the tense silence could drag on any longer, Essie gave an exaggerated yawn, shifted closer to Farrendel, and plunked her head onto his shoulder, tucking her feet onto the cushion. "I think I'm going to take a nap."

Weylind made a tiny, strangled sound at the sight of

them snuggling. When Farrendel risked a peek at them, Jalissa's eyes had widened, and even Rheva had frozen.

Farrendel tensed as Essie squirmed and wiggled, trying to find a comfortable spot on his shoulder.

If they had been alone, he would have wrapped his arm around her and tucked her against him, as he had done during their long nights after one of his nightmares.

But, with his family watching, all he did was tilt his shoulder a bit until Essie gave that sigh of pleasure and snuggled into place. After a few minutes, her breathing began to even out as she drifted off to sleep.

"Is she asleep?" Weylind eyed Essie with something between disgust and puzzlement. He spoke in elvish, probably believing Essie would not be able to understand him even if she was still awake. Not that Farrendel was about to tell him how competent Essie was becoming at understanding elvish.

Besides, based on the way Essie was slumped against his shoulder, Essie was likely asleep. So when Farrendel replied, it was not a lie. "Yes."

Next to him, Ryfon and Brina were edging away, as if seeing their uncle snuggling was making them uncomfortable.

But considering how unwelcoming his family had been to Essie, Farrendel did not care how uncomfortable his family was. He was in the mood to rub his relationship with Essie in their faces, if that was what it took for them to finally recognize that Essie was exactly what he needed all along.

"Do you care for her, shashon?" Jalissa eyed him and Essie, snuggled as they were.

For a moment, Farrendel thought about attempting to roll his eyes like Essie did. The whole snuggled up together thing should have given away how much he cared for Essie. He would not let her this close otherwise.

Instead, he remained mature. Quiet sincerity would go over better. "Yes. She does not mind my scars."

His feelings for her went far deeper than just her lack of disgust at his scars. But it was a simple way to put it that his family would understand.

Rheva's eyes softened, and the supportive nod she sent Farrendel's way indicated that perhaps not all of his family was so torn when it came to Essie.

Weylind's jaw worked, his eyes still a little flinty. But he did not speak, thankfully.

Jalissa sighed, her eyes pained. "We do not mind your scars either."

"Not like her. She..." Farrendel trailed off, as he looked down at where Essie slept against him. How could he possibly convey to his family the way Essie saw *him* in a way that even they did not? "They do not bother her."

"Of course they bother me. You are my little brother. I held you as an infant. I dried your tears when you were a child." Jalissa leaned forward, even more pain shimmering in her dark brown eyes. "It hurts to see my little brother hurt."

"I know." Farrendel had to look away. He knew his family loved him and worried for him, but it was hard to carry the burden of their hurt for him on top of his own struggles.

"That is why I do not want to see you hurt by her. I want you to be happy." Jalissa's voice held a depth of pain, as if she had experience being hurt.

Though if she had, she had never told Farrendel about it.

Still, he was sick and tired of his family doubting

Essie, no matter their reasons. Yes, they worried for him. Yes, they had good reason to doubt. But this was Essie, and even if they doubted Farrendel, it was not right that they could not see Essie for the wonderful, caring person that she was.

"She makes me happy." Farrendel stated it firmly, meeting Jalissa's gaze.

"Does she care for you?" Jalissa countered, her eyes intense.

Weylind and Rheva seemed content to remain out of it, while Ryfon and Brina huddled on the bench as if they really wished they were somewhere else.

"It has only been two and a half months." Farrendel did not want his family to keep questioning Essie like this. Why could they not let her and Farrendel find their way in peace?

"That did not stop you from caring."

No, it had not. But how could he help caring for Essie when she was the warmest, most caring person he had ever met? Of course he cared for her. Besides, she was his wife. Caring for her was kind of the point, was it not?

He could hear Weylind's admonition from before the wedding. *You love too easily.* But, perhaps, this was one time when that was not a bad thing. Farrendel and Essie were married. Far better that they learned to care for each other quickly rather than waste time being miserable. Essie had shown him that.

Farrendel raised his head and met first Jalissa's gaze, then Weylind's, putting a firm conviction into his words. "I believe she does."

Weylind opened his mouth, but Rheva rested her hand on his arm, speaking before he had a chance. "Of course she does. We all can see how happy you are together, and I, for one, am thankful to see it."

Rheva's words were spoken with that finality that kept even Weylind from continuing the conversation.

Farrendel tilted his head in a slight nod to Rheva. At least one of the members of his family had accepted Essie. Well, two. Machasheni Leyleira had taken to Essie right away.

For several long moments, everyone lapsed into silence. Farrendel shifted, trying to move his arm without waking Essie. Perhaps he should join Essie in dozing. Once she woke, she would be wide-awake late tonight, and he would likely be kept awake talking with her.

Yet unlike Essie, he could not bring himself to sleep with so many people around, even if those people were his family and he trusted them.

With Essie sleeping against him, he could not pass the time by exercising on the top of the train. Nor did he want to try to start up another conversation with his family, given the direction the last conversation had taken.

Instead, he glanced at Ryfon and Brina. "Would you care for a game of eshalma?"

Ryfon blinked at Farrendel. Brina gaped, then grinned. "You want to play? With us? It has been so long since you asked to play a game."

Had it? Farrendel tried to remember the last time he had offered to play a game with his niece and nephew and failed. He had gotten into such a habit of retreating to spend the time by himself rather than with his family. He just had not had the energy to spend on people for such a long time.

After another stunned moment, Brina hopped to her

feet, then crouched to dig through the drawer underneath the seat where the games were kept. She located the game, shut the drawer, and returned to her seat.

Ryfon got out the pieces for the table, then glanced toward Farrendel.

Farrendel felt another smile ease onto his face, and he stretched his arm out. "I cannot move. You will need to set it up where I can reach."

But that meant Weylind's legs were currently in the way.

"Dacha? Could you move?" Ryfon juggled the pieces of the table as he glanced at his parents.

Weylind glanced up from his paperwork. Then, Rheva tapped his arm, and together the two of them slid along the bench so that they were out of the way.

Ryfon set up the table, and Brina laid out the board and started on the pieces.

Jalissa eased closer. "Do you mind if I join?"

"No. The game is better with four." Ryfon's smile widened.

Also smiling, Brina began setting up a fourth set of pieces.

Farrendel's own smile remained in place as they started playing. He had not even realized how much he had missed truly spending time with his family like this.

CHAPTER

SEVENTEEN

A s their horses rounded the bend in the trail and the clearing around Lethorel and its small lake opened in front of them, Farrendel kept his gaze on Essie to catch the moment she saw Lethorel.

She did not disappoint. Her resting smile turned into a wide grin, and her eyes sparkled as she glanced at him. "Can we race around the lake? Ashenifela is itching for a run."

Her voice and eyes held a laughing challenge. He found himself smiling back, a long-buried sense of mischief stirring in his chest. He urged his horse into a gallop without waiting for her to call a start.

From behind him, he heard her laugh before Ashenifela's hooves pounded after him.

As they rounded the bend around the lake, Ashenifela pulled alongside him, and Essie's wild laughter rang out on the breeze that tossed her red hair. Farrendel found himself watching her more than where they were going as they flashed into the yard at the base of the massive willow tree that formed Lethorel, and only his quick reflexes saved him when he nearly didn't see a low hanging branch that would have smacked him in the face if he had not ducked.

His horse skidded to a halt, snorting and prancing after the run. He hopped down from his horse, but he was still not fast enough to lift Essie down. Instead, she had swung down and given her mare a kiss on the nose, petting the horse's neck and crooning to her.

When his family, the guards, and the servants caught up, one of the servants claimed his horse's reins, then Ashenifela's. Essie watched the servant take the horse away, looking a bit heartbroken to be torn from her new pet so soon.

"You like that horse."

She started and turned to him, her smile a bit lopsided. "Yes."

"Then she is yours." Farrendel would make it happen. It should not be hard. Ashenifela was one of the horses that his family kept in the town of Arorien. He would simply have to let the rest of his family know that Ashenifela was officially Essie's from now on. He did not think anyone else had claimed the mare.

Essie's smile widened, warm and bright in that way that made his head spin a bit.

He held out his hand, trying to sound normal and not like her smile made him tongue-tied. "Would you like to see our rooms?"

Essie clasped his fingers in the elven manner, thankfully, since his family were all but gawking at them at this point. Not that Farrendel cared with Essie still smiling at him. She tugged him toward Lethorel. "Yes, please."

Farrendel led the way up the spiraling staircase grown

into the broad base of the willow tree. As he climbed, something inside him eased, as if the weight of the war and who he had become as Laesornysh melted away here at Lethorel.

Instead of battle and bloodshed, this place was filled with some of his most cherished memories. Long, golden days spent with his dacha. Laughter as Jalissa attempted to teach him archery. The weeks during the summer when his whole family would be here and, for those few weeks, everything was perfect.

Essie gaped as they walked deeper into Lethorel. Trailing branches formed curtains of fluttering leaves all around them, making each room private and cozy. Just like at Ellonahshinel, his rooms were all the way at the farthest reaches of the branches, yet at Lethorel, the smaller set of rooms were tucked into a haven of trailing branches, lit green from the sun glowing through the surrounding leaves.

The small cottage perched on the branch with just a small porch in front of the door. The porch was held up by posts formed of living branches still sprouting leaves.

Essie's steps staggered, and she gripped him more tightly for a moment. When he glanced down at her, she smiled, her eyes wide and bright. "It's beautiful."

Farrendel smiled, and the expression felt more real and genuine than it had in a long time. The smile remained in place, almost painful with disuse, as he opened the door and tugged Essie inside.

The small sitting room was only big enough for a couple of chairs and a small kitchen area formed of cupboards along one wall. Two doors on the far wall led to the two small bedrooms.

Essie waved at the doors across the way. "Is your

room on the right and mine on the left like at home or do we switch it up here?"

He opened his mouth to answer, then Essie's words stuck in his head.

Home. It was a word that he usually applied to Lethorel. And Essie used to refer to the home she had left behind in Escarland when she had married him.

But, this time, she had called Ellonahshinel *home*.

Essie's eyebrows scrunched as she studied him. "What? Is something wrong?"

He could not meet her gaze, his heart beating faster. "You called Estyra home."

"Of course I did. It's home." She squeezed the two fingers that she still had clasped in hers. "I mean it. I love Estyra. I love our rooms there. I love so much of my new life."

His brain felt like it was fizzling again. She had used the L-word about Estyra and their home and their life.

Did that mean that she...that they...

He had *felt* more around her, and those feelings had only been growing and deepening.

Would he call them...would he dare use that word when it came to her?

He forced the smile back to his face. He had to act normal, not like she was shaking him to the core. "You can take your pick if you would like."

Her smile playing across her face, Essie shook her head. "I know you. You like your routines and habits. Your room is usually the one on the right, isn't it?"

Without thinking, a laugh bubbled in his chest and burst out before he had a chance to stop it. Somehow, Essie had him figured out, for sure. "Yes, it is."

"Then I'll take the room on the left." Essie let go of Farrendel's hand and headed for the door.

Farrendel remained frozen in place, staring after Essie even once she had shut the door behind her.

It was time to trust her with the truth of himself—of his illegitimacy. Then, once that was done, he would trust her with his heart.

His heart pounded harder just thinking about it. If he let himself fall in love with her, then she would have the power to break him beyond repair.

But this was Essie. He was well on his way to falling in love with her *because* he could trust her with his heart. She would not hurt him.

No, it was time to tell her that he loved her. And, maybe, before they left Lethorel, he might even work up the courage to kiss her.

FARRENDEL SAT with his back to their cottage, his arm around Essie. She snuggled against him, a blanket around her shoulders.

The day had been nearly as wonderful as he had hoped. He had mildly panicked when Essie had jumped into the lake with what she had called a *cannonball*. But the water fight had erased the panic with her laughter.

And then Weylind had gotten a message that the trolls had raided the border. But as long as the raids remained minor, they would not call for Farrendel's help. It was tough, but he was trying to put thoughts of the war and possibly getting called away out of his mind so he could enjoy the evening.

He should tell her that he was illegitimate. The two of them were alone. He would not get a better opportunity.

Yet he could not bring himself to break the quiet relaxation of this moment with something as serious as that.

Perhaps he should instead tell her that he was falling in love with her. But he could not confess that until he confessed his illegitimacy.

And that left him stuck in silence.

The evening faded into the gray of twilight as the last light of the sunset disappeared from between the trees.

"I can see why you love this place so much." Essie's head remained pillowed on his shoulder as she spoke. "It is beautiful. And peaceful."

Down below, a light flickered along the lake. Then another light flashed and winked out.

Essie lifted her head for a moment. "Fireflies!"

Farrendel nodded, a smile tugging at his mouth. He had known Essie would love the fireflies here at Lethorel. "Yes."

Essie rested her head against his shoulder again as more fireflies winked all along the lakeside among the trees. More fireflies blinked in the willow branches of Lethorel, a host of tiny dots of light among the darkening forest. A magic that was peaceful and natural, unlike Farrendel's magic.

Another thing he had yet to tell Essie. What would she think when she saw his magic? Worse, what would she think when she found out just how deadly he was when he used it? She knew he was Laesornysh. But a vague knowing was different than *knowing*.

Perhaps he would never have to show her that part of himself. He did his best to keep the Laesornysh part of himself isolated at the border, even if it still seeped into his entire life despite his best efforts.

"Farrendel?" Essie tilted her face up to peer at him.

He realized that he had stiffened. He forced his muscles to relax. "I am fine."

"You were thinking about the trolls and the message Weylind received, weren't you?" Essie reached over and took his hand.

Close enough. He nodded and squeezed her fingers. "I am enjoying the evening. It is just..."

"You worry. I am learning how your mind works." She patted his chest, a gesture she had been doing more often lately. He was not sure what had made her start, but he appreciated it. Her touch drew his attention to her and out of whatever spiraling thoughts had taken over his head at any given moment.

He was thankful that she did not seem bothered by the fact that his mind had wandered down darker trails even though they were supposed to be enjoying a romantic evening.

But he was not very good at anything that could be termed "romantic." Before Essie, he had never had a reason to attempt it.

He cleared his throat and gestured at the dancing fireflies down below. "This is pretty."

Essie gave a soft laugh and looked down at the lake reflecting the glittering fireflies. "It is."

For the first year ever, Farrendel almost wished his family was not here at Lethorel with him. With the darkness descending around them, Farrendel could almost pretend that he and Essie were alone here at Lethorel, enjoying the wedding trip that they had never bothered to have.

Even with his family here, he was determined to make the most of this time at Lethorel.

He and Essie sat in the growing dark for a while longer before Essie heaved a sigh. "I suppose we should head for bed. Breakfast will be far too early in the morning."

At a normal time in the morning, at least for Farrendel. But Essie preferred to sleep later into the morning.

He stood, pulling Essie up with him. She opened the door to the cottage and stepped inside first, though she did not release his hand. Not yet.

Inside their darkened sitting room, Farrendel halted. This was it. It was a romantic night. He should kiss her.

Essie faced him, standing only inches away. When he eased closer, she did not step away. Instead, she tipped her face toward his, as if she was hoping he would kiss her.

His breath caught, and his muscles locked. He could not seem to make himself move those last few inches.

It was not as if he did not *want* to kiss her. He did. Very much.

But that was the problem. He wanted to kiss her. But he wanted to do it right.

He had never kissed anyone before. What if he did it wrong? Would he even know if he were doing it wrong? He did not want to mess this up. Not with Essie. She meant too much to him.

Essie's mouth quirked with something that seemed torn between amusement and disappointment. She swayed, as if she intended to pull back.

He had been frozen too long, letting his worries take over again.

With a deep breath, he leaned forward. At the last

moment, he took the coward's way out and kissed her forehead. "Goodnight."

And then…he fled.

FARRENDEL ATTEMPTED TO READ A BOOK, but he was too distracted. A little farther along the shoreline, Essie and Brina relaxed on the moss, chatting, their hair still wet after swimming. From this distance, Farrendel could not hear what they were saying. But the bright looks on both of their faces eased something inside him. It was good to see someone in his family interacting with Essie.

Farther along the way, Rheva and Jalissa talked quietly, also enjoying the warmth and sunlight.

Footsteps scuffed the gravel a moment before Weylind dropped to the ground next to Farrendel. When Farrendel glanced at Weylind, the tense, strained lines around Weylind's mouth seemed out of place for the relaxation they had enjoyed the past few days.

Farrendel straightened, his chest tightening. "What is wrong?"

This was it. He was going to get called away. Instead of three weeks at Lethorel, he had only gotten three days.

Weylind glanced at the others and, when he spoke, he kept his voice low. "There was another raid at the border. But this time, the trolls did not retreat. They disappeared deeper into the forest, and the border patrols have yet to locate them."

"How many?" This was worse than Farrendel had feared. A large group of trolls could wreak havoc on inno-cent towns and villages. It was bad enough when warriors died in the fighting. But when innocents died in their homes, that hit even harder.

"The scouts estimate about a hundred." Weylind's tone remained flat and hard. Though, when Rheva glanced in their direction, he smiled and nodded as if nothing was wrong.

"When do I leave?" Farrendel stared at the lake in front of him. Everything in him was already growing cold, knowing he was headed back to war.

"You are not leaving. Not yet." Weylind's shoulders lifted in a small shrug. "The scouts and patrols are still trying to locate the trolls. I have ordered reinforcements to guard the towns in the area where the troll warriors were last seen. Until we have more information, there is nothing either of us can do."

That might be true, but Farrendel did not like sitting here, knowing danger was out there stalking the innocents of his kingdom.

Yet he did not want to leave either.

"We will keep it quiet for now. There is no reason to alarm the others yet." Weylind speared Farrendel with a sharp look, brooking no argument. "We will quietly step up our patrols in the forest around Lethorel. I do not think the trolls will come this far into Tarenhiel, nor do they know the location of Lethorel, but we should stay alert."

Farrendel glanced at Essie, where she was still smiling and laughing in blissful ignorance. He did not want to keep this from Essie. He was not sure if he could keep his added tension from her.

But he did not want to ruin this time at Lethorel. He was getting so close to working up the courage to tell her about his illegitimacy. Maybe even tell her about his magic. And finally kiss her. Properly kiss her, rather than just on her forehead.

"All right. I will not tell Essie." Farrendel clenched and unclenched his fingers, trying to relax. He had not buckled on his swords that morning, and now his back itched with the lack of their comforting weight. Hopefully Essie would not think anything of it if he started wearing his swords around Lethorel. He wore them often enough around Estyra.

Weylind nodded, his own hands clenched far too tightly before his fingers and posture relaxed. "Try to enjoy our remaining time at Lethorel. I do not know what the trolls are planning, but I fear it will not be long before they reveal their scheme."

All summer, things had been off. The trolls had conducted those mysterious raids, the ones where they seemed to be trying to avoid the border patrols instead of engage them. And now this. A small army of troll warriors had disappeared inside Tarenhiel.

This was not the same war they had been fighting for the past few years. The trolls were planning something bigger, something more decisive.

And it would be up to Farrendel to stop them.

He released a long breath and let his head hang for a moment. This happiness with Essie was so fleeting. Weylind said to enjoy this time they had, but was it worth it, knowing how soon it would be over?

Or, perhaps, that was the very reason he should savor it?

Before Essie, he would have already shut down and turned to ice.

But now, he had her to think about. He struggled to

hope for a future, but he could not help but reach for the hope he saw in her eyes.

She hoped for a future where the tension between Escarland and Tarenhiel no longer existed. Where the two kingdoms together could bring about peace for Tarenhiel. And, most of all, a future for the two of them.

Could he both fight the trolls and fight for a future with Essie? He was not sure he had the strength to do both.

EIGHTEEN

F arrendel stretched his magical senses deeper into the forest around him, searching for anything amiss. His swords rested against his back, ready if needed.

Not that he was searching for anything specifically. The hundred troll warriors had yet to be located. For all the scouts knew, the trolls had returned to Kostaria.

Yet why would they have returned just as quietly as they had entered, without raiding so much as a single village? Was this simply a larger version of those smaller, mysterious raids? If so, then what was the purpose? The trolls were not sneaking in and out of Tarenhiel for no reason.

But figuring out their reasons was Weylind's problem. And a problem for all the generals and experts.

Farrendel's job was simply to fight the enemy wherever they showed up and protect his people.

He crept to the next tree, still searching the

surrounding forest with his senses. As he kept moving, something icy sliced against his instincts.

He froze, pressing his back against a tree, as he probed his senses farther in that direction. There was something there. Something that did not belong in the green and earth of the forest.

Ice. Stone. And troll magic.

Farrendel waited another moment just to be sure he was really sensing the pack of trolls headed toward Lethorel. They were not just a figment of his overactive senses. But no. They were really there. Sharper now in his senses. Coming fast.

He spun and raced toward Lethorel. Toward where Essie had said she would be practicing archery with Jalissa that morning.

Essie. She was here. In the path of a hundred trolls.

He dashed around the trees until he reached the archery range. Jalissa and Essie stood at the far end, and Jalissa's hand froze in the process of reaching for another arrow. He skidded to a halt next to them. "Get inside. Now."

As much as he wanted to stay at Essie's side, he could not wait for them to follow his orders. He had to alert Weylind and their guards so that they could set up their defense.

Would any defense be enough? There were a hundred trolls—maybe more, if the estimate was wrong—on their way. And they had only Weylind, Farrendel, and ten guards to face them.

Farrendel would have to use his magic. Not just use it but unleash it. There would be no help for it, not if he wanted to protect Essie and his family.

As Farrendel raced into the clearing at the base of Lethorel, Weylind turned toward him, his jaw tightening, before he spun back toward Rheva, Ryfon, and Brina. "Hurry. Get inside."

Farrendel halted by the cluster of guards, led by Iyrinder. "A pack of trolls is coming. I did not stay to see how many."

Iyrinder nodded, then started giving orders, assembling the guards in front of Lethorel.

As they stepped into their places, Essie and Jalissa hurried past them, their arms laden with arrows. They started up the stairs into Lethorel before Farrendel had a chance to say anything to Essie.

He was not sure what he would have said or done, even if he had the chance. It was not like he was going to kiss her now, with his family gawking and a pack of trolls bearing down on them.

At least she would be as safe as possible in Lethorel. As she and Jalissa disappeared in the main room nestled in the branches, the guards walled the stairs off with a thick layer of branches, turning Lethorel into as much of a fortress as they could manage.

The icy taste of troll magic rammed into Farrendel's senses a moment before the first, faint sounds of the trolls' howling war chants floated to him on the breeze.

Weylind drew his sword, a longer, larger blade than the ones Farrendel carried. His jaw was tight, his dark eyes hard. "Farrendel, shashon..."

"I know." Farrendel nodded. Weylind did not have to say it. Farrendel knew what he would have to do.

As the growling chant grew louder, Farrendel faced that direction. He had only Weylind and ten guards at his back. None of them had their fighting leathers or more than a few, cursory weapons. If they were going to survive, then Farrendel would need to be brutal and merciless with his magic.

He shoved aside any thoughts of fear, of Essie, of happiness. All he felt was ice. Steel. Death.

The first couple of trolls stepped out of the tree line. They were dressed for war in their leather armor studded with stone. Axes and swords flashed in the mid-morning sunlight.

Farrendel stalked forward and drew his swords. With a deep breath, he released his magic, and it crackled down the length of his swords. More of his magic shivered around him, filling the air with a humming. The power prickled along his scalp.

The trolls howled one last time before they charged at him, swinging their weapons.

Farrendel took two running steps and launched himself at them. His magic-laced swords carved through the first two trolls. As he dove deeper into the pack of trolls, he shoved bolts of his magic outward, blasting more of the trolls.

Lunging into the air, Farrendel plunged his swords into two more trolls, flipped in the air, and sliced through two more trolls as he came down.

An ax flashed, aimed at his foot, and Farrendel blasted the ax—and the troll holding it—with his magic.

A gun boomed—a weapon rarely found in the hands of someone other than a human—but the bullet just sparked into nothing as Farrendel's magic incinerated it.

Each gulp of breath tasted of gunpowder, blood, and magic. Farrendel could not let himself think. He could not feel.

His magic surged within him, and more and more of it slipped past his control to whirl around him in a destructive torrent. He struggled to hold it in check. He could not let it burst out of his control, or it would destroy a swathe of the forest—and Lethorel and everyone sheltering inside.

As he struggled with his grip on his building power, some of the trolls circled, trying to get behind him. Before they could get far, arrows slammed into them.

Farrendel had to end this before he lost control. He lashed into the remaining trolls and, even as their fellow warriors fell around them, they kept fighting rather than surrender. An arrow claimed one. Farrendel's power blasted another. Then he drove his sword into the chest of the remaining troll.

As the troll's body fell, Farrendel drew in his magic, stuffing it back deep inside. It fought, burning in his chest, before he got it quenched.

He lowered his swords, tiredness shaking through his muscles.

What was Essie thinking, as she watched him kill? As she stared down from Lethorel and saw him now, covered in the blood and gore of battle?

He could not face her. Not now.

His throat was closing. His chest tightening.

After spinning on his heels, he dashed for a stand of brush around the corner of the lake, where he would be hidden from sight.

At the edge of the lake, he crashed to his knees and dropped his swords. His hands shook, and he could not yank off his belt, tunic, and shirt fast enough.

So dirty. So blood-spattered and filthy.

He plunged his hands and his shirt into the cold water

of the lake. The cold should have steadied him, but he gasped for breath, his whole body shaking. He could not be sick. He could not lose it. Not now.

Yet he was breaking anyway. He was not strong enough to hold himself together.

"Farrendel? It's me. Essie."

No. He froze. No, Essie could not see him like this.

"Leave." The word rasped out. Harsh. Desperate.

"Farrendel, I'm not leaving you." Essie's steps were slow and deliberate, telling him exactly where she was as she walked around the bushes even though he could not bring himself to look at her.

He clenched his shirt in his hands, a desperate paralysis gripping him. "Leave. Please."

She had to go away. Any moment now, he would go back to breaking. And he could not let her see that. He could not let her see him like *this*.

"I will go if you truly want me to. But please know you don't have to be alone. I'm here for you." Her voice was low and soothing.

He tried to steady his breathing as her words seeped into him. She was standing there, not leaving, even though he was hunched here, spattered with the blood of those he had killed. He had tried pushing her away, and yet she had not flinched.

He had intended to trust her with his secrets while they were here at Lethorel. It seemed he would be trusting her with far more than he had planned.

Hunching, he gave in to the shaking. With trembling hands, he scrubbed his shirt over his arms, trying to rinse the blood from his skin.

The pebbles of the beach shifted as Essie crept nearer, then knelt next to him.

Her nearness just made his skin crawl with how dirty he was. He scrubbed harder, trying to get the feel of blood and gore off his skin.

It did not matter how hard he scrubbed. He could still feel the blood. The filth. His breathing hitched, his brain whirling.

Essie's hand rested on his, halting him.

He glanced at her, but she was a blur in the black tunnel closing around him. His breaths came faster, shuddering through his whole body. He opened his mouth, trying to explain but not sure if the words came out coherent. "I can't...can't get clean."

"I know. I know." Essie's voice remained that soothing, steady tone. "Let me help."

Her fingers gently pried his shirt from his grip. He shuddered and squeezed his eyes shut. It was all he could do to breathe in and out.

Water dripped, then Essie swiped the cold, damp shirt against his jaw. She scrubbed along his jaw, up his cheek, and then his ear. The cold of the damp shirt was a grounding shock, steadying him the longer she worked.

He wrangled his breathing under control, until he was able to open his eyes and glance at Essie. Her green eyes were wide but filled with a depth of concern that shook him and held him together at the same time.

Slowly, he reached up and rested his fingers over her hand where she had been dabbing at the blood on his neck. "I have been dreading the day you would see my magic. I did not know how you would react. My magic is not..." It was not beautiful. Not wonderful and magical like most elven power. "Most have magic that grows and creates. Mine destroys."

Instead of flinching away from him, Essie held his gaze. "Your magic protects. There is no shame in that."

Was there not? Here he was, covered in the blood of his enemies. Yet no hint of disgust crossed her face.

Still holding his gaze, she traced her thumb over his cheek. "I care about you, Farrendel Laesornysh. All of you. Your magic and all."

His breath caught, his heart beating harder.

He could not embrace this acceptance from her. Not when she did not yet know the truth. He hung his head, staring at his hands. "You do not know everything about me. I…"

How could he explain? The words choked in his throat. This was not the right time and place for this conversation.

"I know." Essie's touch on his cheek brought his gaze back to hers. She spoke with certainty, not just a soothing reassurance.

"You know?" He searched her face, his muscles stiffening. How would she know? Who had told her? Did she know what she thought she knew? "That I am a…" He switched to elvish and spat the word. He did not think Essie would know it. He certainly had not taught it to her.

But he had learned it at a young age. He had had it spat at him far too often when he was growing up. Even now, the nobles whispered it when they thought Weylind would not hear.

"Your grandmother told me. On my third day here." Essie did not wince, even at the way he had spat the derogatory term for his birth.

Of course Machasheni had told Essie. No one else would be that plain-spoken, but Machasheni Leyleira was not ruffled by such delicate topics.

He could no longer hold Essie's gaze. He slumped, staring off over the lake. "I am sorry."

"Why are you sorry?" Essie cradled his face in both of her hands, her touch soft. "It's not your fault, Farrendel. None of the mistakes are yours. You can't help how you were born."

"I am still tainted." Farrendel held up his hands. Even after all his scrubbing, blood still crusted beneath his fingernails and in the creases of his palms.

The taint of his birth clung to him just as much. And since Essie was married to him, it would cling to her too.

Essie's voice dropped low with conviction, as if she willed him to heed her words. "You are your father's son, no matter how it happened. He acknowledged you and raised you as one of the family, as you deserve to be. That makes you a prince of the elves. No matter your magic. No matter your birth. No matter what anyone says. You are not tainted."

Her words were nothing new. His dacha had told him the exact same thing many times. So had Weylind and Rheva and the rest of his family.

But he had already known his family loved him, no matter what. It was different, hearing the reassurance from Essie.

He had trusted her with all of his secrets and brokenness, and she still cared. She still sat there, cradling his face with a gentle touch.

As his muscles relaxed, he took her hand. "Linshi."

"Of course." Essie sat back on her heels. "Your brother said to talk to him as soon as you were ready. He sounded serious. Well, more serious than usual."

Right. Now that Farrendel could think again, it struck him how easy that fight had been. Sure, he had killed quite a few trolls. But there had been nowhere near a hundred in that attack.

And that meant seventy or more trolls were still out there. This attack was not over.

NINETEEN

F arrendel stretched his senses as he led the column of riders along the thin path from Lethorel back to Arorien. Somewhere out there, seventy or more trolls were lurking. Had they set up an ambush or had they headed to Estyra?

Either way, Farrendel was not sure that taking to the road and making for Arorien was the wisest decision. He would have preferred to remain at Lethorel where Essie and the other non-warriors in the group could remain safe in a fortified position. Surely the trolls would have come to them eventually. Or someone would have noticed that the king was no longer sending messages along the root system and gone to investigate. They would have soon discovered the root system had been cut, and Weylind was holed up at Lethorel.

But Weylind was worried for the rest of the kingdom. Who knew what seventy trolls could get up to if left to their own devices? The trolls might plan another, even larger offensive raid into Tarenhiel, knowing they had the king and his best warrior bottled up at Lethorel.

While staying at Lethorel would be safer for Essie, leaving was better for Tarenhiel. So Weylind made the decision to risk the road.

Farrendel resisted the urge to glance over his shoulder to search out Essie in the riders behind him. He needed to stay focused ahead and around them. He could not afford to miss the slightest sign of trouble.

She would be fine. He would make sure of it. Besides, she had claimed two guns and an armload of ammunition from the dead trolls who had attacked Lethorel. Farrendel had never seen her shoot a gun, but she had seemed confident in the way she handled the weapons.

They rode in silence. Only the soft clop of hooves on the sandy gravel of the trail, the faint creak of leather, and the occasional whuffle from one of the horses broke the quiet of the forest.

As they rounded a bend, the familiar sense of boulders deeper in the forest ahead brushed against his instincts. He never liked this part of the trail, where large boulders in the forest pressed against his magic.

Yet this time, something jangled. He held up his hand, reining in his horse and stretching his senses toward the rocks that hid just out of sight of the trail. Behind him, snorting and stamping came from the horses as the others halted.

There was something there. Something...

"Down!" Farrendel dove from his horse. Even as he urged his horse to the ground with one hand, he sent a bolt of his magic into the air. A gunshot echoed as his magic sizzled the bullet into nothing.

A howling war chant roared from the forest ahead. At

least Farrendel had sensed them before he and his family had ridden between the boulders, where they would have been surrounded by the trolls.

The trolls burst from their hiding spots and crashed into sight, dodging around trees and hefting their weapons as they ran.

Farrendel held his ground, waiting for them to come to him. Behind him, the others were hastily urging their horses to lie down in a circle, growing a sapling wall for protection, and nocking arrows to their bowstrings.

Farrendel drew his swords and unleashed more of his magic, letting it crackle outward from him until he shielded those behind him.

Gunshots echoed from the forest, and the bullets fizzled as his magic incinerated them, filling the air with the stench of overheated metal.

A troll leapt over a log and lunged at Farrendel. With ice filling his veins and heart, Farrendel dodged the troll's ax and sliced his sword across his neck. Springing off the falling body, he launched himself into the air. As he came down, he used his momentum to drive a sword into another troll's chest.

Even as he fought with his swords, he let his magic blast around him, slicing through far more trolls with his magic than he did with his swords. More and more of it begged to be released, and he eased his control a fraction to send bolts of his magic extending in all directions, protecting Essie and his family hunkered in their defensive circle behind him.

His power lashed the trees around him, leaving black scars. He was killing the forest. How soon before he accidentally killed those huddled behind him? They were far too close. All it would take was one slip of his control, and he would destroy his family as surely as he destroyed the marauding trolls.

He would simply have to finish this fight before he lost control.

In a blur, he tore into the charging trolls with both swords and magic. The air reeked of the sizzling tang of his power, the metallic taste of blood, and the stench of burned body.

The trolls were circling, going around him to try to reach the others. Elven magic lashed out with roots and tree branches, pummeling the charging trolls.

Troll magic filled the air, hurling stone and ice. It fizzled out against Farrendel's magic, but it battered the wooden defenses of the others. Some of the elven guards popped up, releasing arrows, before they dove back into cover.

Farrendel's magic tore at his control, lashing out in a whirling fury around him. He had to protect them. He had to protect *Essie*.

The trolls kept coming. They were spreading out, trying to escape the reach of his lashing magic to attack Weylind and the others. The elf and troll magic washed back and forth between them, and Farrendel did not dare release more of his magic to help. What if he lost control?

The war howls of the trolls turned into a gruff, rhythmic chanting. It was hard to tell with the trolls' accent, but Farrendel thought they were chanting *Gun, gun, gun.*

Why would they chant *gun*? They had plenty of guns already, far more than Farrendel had ever seen them use in battle before. And these guns seemed different. They could shoot five shots before they needed to be reloaded, and they were not loaded at the muzzle like the guns Farrendel had seen used before.

Yet those guns still made little difference. One shot or five, Farrendel's magic easily incinerated them.

Except...Farrendel peered at the trail ahead at the faint sound of creaking. There, four well-muscled trolls hauled the largest gun Farrendel had ever seen. It was mounted on two wooden wagon wheels and appeared to be made up of a circle of gun barrels banded together. A string of cartridges looped from the gun down to a box while a crank stuck out of one side.

What *was* it? And where had the trolls gotten it from? It did not seem very troll-like in design.

None of that mattered right now. It was a gun, and it was a danger.

Farrendel started running toward it, blasting out with his magic. Yet even as he ran, one of the trolls turned the crank at the side of the gun.

With successive concussions, the gun spat a near continuous line of bullets, aimed directly at Farrendel.

At the same time, all the trolls on the battlefield, now arranged in a semi-circle around him, pivoted and turned their guns and magic on Farrendel.

Farrendel skidded to a halt, yanking his magic in close to absorb the hailstorm of bullets. He had never fought a barrage like this. He could fend off axes and swords and berserking trolls, but he did not have experience fighting off so many guns.

A gunshot sounded from behind him. Had the trolls gotten behind him? Were they shooting at Essie and his family?

His magic faltered for a moment. He stumbled down to one knee as a bullet made it through the bolts of his magic and whizzed past his head, clipping a section of his hair.

One of the trolls fell, blood blossoming on his shirt. That gunshot must have been Essie, not one of the trolls.

But his control on his magic had slipped. The shield he had wrapped around himself had loosened, and he scrambled to draw the scattering bolts back to himself. More bullets whizzed past him, cutting far too close.

He had to unleash more power. But his control was already frayed and fragile. More would just burn through his fingers. He could destroy this entire swathe of forest. He could kill Essie if he lost his grip on the magic.

But if he did not release more magic, he could die.

His magic pulsed in his chest, burning down his arms as it begged to be unleashed. To destroy. To kill.

No, he could not risk it. The magic already bursting around him would have to be enough. It did not matter that it was shaking and falling apart under the onslaught of bullets. He did not have the control to handle any more.

Even as he peered through the crackle of his magic, that repeating gun adjusted its aim, the line of bullets changing just a hair. The bullets winked out against his magic until…

Pain slammed into his stomach, and he cried out. The last of his control snapped, and his magic exploded outward, fizzling out on the breeze.

He collapsed the rest of the way to his knees as three spots of blood bloomed on the front of his shirt.

He had been shot. He had never been shot before. Each breath stabbed more pain through his body, and his head whirled in a way he had never experienced before.

Gunshots echoed around him. The battlefield around

him blurred in a haze of troll and elf magic, sulfuric gun smoke, and a ringing…ringing…

That ringing was in his head. His heartbeat pounded in his ears as the blood poured from his wounds.

He had to…he had to get up. He had to fight.

His magic. He needed his magic.

A few bolts shivered into existence around him. He forced more of it outward, taking out the bullets flying through the air.

The repeater gun had fallen silent. All of the trolls who had been manning it lay dead on the ground.

A gun boomed, and a troll charging at Farrendel collapsed. Farrendel sought the source and found Essie. She lay behind Ashenifela and a low wall of saplings. Her red hair frizzed from its braid, the tendrils whipping about her face in the breeze. She held out her gun to his niece Brina, and Brina handed a second gun to her. With her jaw set, Essie put the gun to her shoulder and lined up her shot. In the months since they had married, he had never seen her eyes that flinty or her bearing that determined.

In that moment, she was a warrior, unflinching at the battle raging around her.

The trolls charged at the others. Sunlight glinted on drawn swords and raised guns for one last volley.

Farrendel hunched, gasping, protected by the bolts of his remaining magic. Blood poured from him. Too fast. Was he dying? It seemed impossible, after everything he had endured, that three bullets could end him just like that.

Yet here he was, bleeding out on a battlefield, while the trolls rushed at Essie and his family.

Weylind fended off waves of troll magic, his black hair

whipping around his shoulders. Rheva crawled between the wounded, keeping her head down as bullets zipped over them now that Farrendel's magic no longer protected them. Jalissa pressed her hands to the ground, her face twisted as she held a section of the protecting wall of saplings in place even as it was riddled with bullets.

Next to her, Ryfon drew a sword, his hands shaking. This was Ryfon's first taste of real battle, yet he was preparing to go down fighting.

Farrendel had been Ryfon's age when he had begged to join Dacha and Weylind at the front. He had thought himself old enough, yet looking at Ryfon now, Farrendel saw the young boy he had been. He had been far too young when he had learned to fight, to kill, to survive torture.

Farther along the circle, Brina loaded another gun for Essie. His niece was even younger than Ryfon, yet her face was set with determination as she handed the gun off to Essie.

And then there was Essie. She raised her gun again, even as the trolls closed to fifteen feet away. Ten feet.

Farrendel staggered to his feet and stumbled toward her. Her gaze swung from its deadly focus on the rampaging trolls to instead rest on him with a pained finality.

He should have kissed her. He should have told her that he was falling in love with her. He had thought he would have more time, and yet now time had narrowed to this moment.

No. No, he would not let this be the end. Not for Essie. Maybe he was dying. But she could not. She had to live.

She had to keep smiling and keep bringing light and joy to a world filled with blood and war.

His magic welled inside him, a rising tide that burst from him. This time, he did not try to hold back the surge. He was going to destroy each and every troll if it was the last thing he did.

He went down to a knee and unleashed his magic. Crackles built in his chest, beneath his skin, until they tore from him. Power gushed from him in a torrent that tugged at his hair and scraped at his clothes. He drew in ragged breaths of pain and power as the weight of his own magic squeezed his chest.

Around him, the trees groaned, as if in pain at his magic. The remaining trolls cried out. But it was already too late for them, as his magic ripped them apart in its fury.

And still his magic blasted from him, wild and raw and tearing at the air itself. It burned through his fingers, growing in strength even as he weakened, and his control along with him. His mind was whirling and fuzzy with blood loss.

He had to keep control. He was supposed to save Essie, not kill her.

Gritting his teeth, Farrendel moaned as he tightened his grasp on his unleashed power. He had to get it under control. Just for a moment more, and then this would all be over.

With a cry of pain that was lost in the thunder of his magic, he gathered in his magic and shoved it at the sky. It exploded with a boom that shook the ground and snapped the nearby trees. The last of it dissipated into the sky, fizzling out in a rain of ash and smoke.

As his magic left, weakness slammed into him until all

his bones and muscles felt dead as the trolls lying in heaps around him.

He sought out Essie, catching her gaze where she still huddled, gripping her gun but very much alive.

She was alive. His family was alive. That was all that mattered.

He let the weakness and darkness take him. It was a relief to collapse to the ground and fade into the darkness. No more fighting. No more blood and battle.

Then she was there, her hands pressing to his stomach. She mumbled something through her tears, but he was too tired to concentrate on the words.

If this was the end, then he was glad she was here. He gathered his strength and peeled his eyes open to see her one last time. "Essie..." He weakly fumbled for her hand.

She clasped his hand, squeezing hard enough that he could feel it past the tingling numbness in his fingers. "Don't die. Please don't die. I love you, Farrendel. I can't..."

She loved him. He could die now. Happy that he had been loved.

His breath hissed out of him, and he did not fight to draw in another breath. Essie was still talking, but he could no longer make out the words. He was fading. After all his years of fighting, it was time to let go.

Something tugged, deep in his chest. Yanking him away from the fading darkness. Away from the death drawing him away. It almost felt like Essie was reaching deep into his heart, begging him to hold on tight to her.

Essie. He had never told her that he loved her. They had a life to live yet.

It was not time to let go. Not time to die. For years, he had gone into battle, not caring if he lived or died.

Yet now that the reality was upon him, he did care. He cared very much.

He reached for that sense of Essie. A breath dragged into his chest. Then another.

The pain slammed back into him, and he gasped. Life flowed back into his fingers, his muscles. And yet the life felt like Essie in a way he could not define.

Then elven healing magic burst into him, tearing at the pain in his stomach. He cried out, yet it seemed he heard Essie's cry of pain too.

Then he was fading into darkness again. A warmer, living darkness wrapped in elven healing magic, even if the pain continued to claw at his middle. Each breath pulled from him, as if forced beyond his will.

He drifted, vaguely aware of movement and voices. The creaking of a litter and the pain as it bumped over roots crossing the path. The snort of horses and the clop of their hooves. And, most of all, Essie's hand in his, warm against his cold fingers.

How long he drifted, he did not know. Some long minutes or hours later, he dragged his way through the darkness and pain as he was lifted from the litter and placed on something hard and flat.

"Farrendel, shashon. You need to wake." Weylind's voice reached deep into his pounding skull, yanking him the rest of the way awake.

Farrendel squinted up into Weylind's blurry, scowling face. He opened his mouth, but he could not seem to get any words out of his dry, sticky mouth.

He became aware of Essie, lying next to him on the large, wooden table, her hand still tightly clasped in his. She was unconscious but in pain.

How did he know that? His heart beat harder as he

searched the new awareness filling his chest. She was in pain and, as his heart hammered in his chest, hers did too. She shifted and whimpered.

Essie. Farrendel struggled to push himself onto an elbow. "Essie…"

Rheva shoved Weylind back and took his place next to the table. She shoved Farrendel back down. "Lie still. You need to take deep, calm breaths."

He lay back and tried to take in a deep breath. Pain lanced through his stomach, and he groaned, pressing a hand to the wounds. Beneath his fingers, he felt rough bandages, sticky with blood. "What…happened?"

"You were shot." Behind Rheva, Weylind crossed his arms, still glowering.

"You are not helping, my love." Rheva half-turned and gently shoved Weylind back another few steps.

An elf Farrendel did not recognize eased into his line of sight. "Adarasheni, if we may proceed?"

"Not yet, but please assemble what we will need." Rheva turned back to Farrendel, resting a hand on his shoulder. A hint of Rheva's soothing magic eased into him, relaxing his muscles.

Next to him, Essie released a sigh, and the pain on her face eased as well. More than that, he *felt* the way her pain eased as his did. What was going on?

The other elf—he must be the healer in Arorien—bustled around the room, setting a pot of water over the fire and setting out the tools for tending a wound.

Farrendel glanced up at Rheva, his fingers tightening over the bandages. "What is it? I am awake. You can safely heal me now."

She would not have been able to do more than stabilize him before he woke up. While he was unconscious, his magic had a tendency to lash out at anyone using magic on him, even those trying to heal him. A side effect of being tortured by troll magic.

A slight smile crossed Rheva's face, at odds with Weylind's continuing scowl. "I would, but you see, you and Elspetha have developed an elishina."

"What?" Farrendel nearly sat upright again but flopped back with a groan. He glanced at Essie, still unconscious next to him, and lifted their clasped hands.

An elishina. That would explain the new awareness of her. He could feel each breath she took, each beat of her heart, deep inside his chest.

Machasheni Leyleira had hinted that an elishina was possible. And Farrendel had dared to hope—in rare moments of optimism—that it might happen for him and Essie. He had even begun to wonder if her rapid learning of elvish might be a sign that the first glimmers of an elishina, the elven heart bond, was happening.

But deep down, he had struggled to hope something that wonderful would happen to him. He had resigned himself to watching Essie live a normal human life, and he had thought it would not matter since he would die young in battle anyway.

Yet he had his chance to die young in battle. And he had not taken it. He had wanted to live, to figure out this new life with Essie, instead. He had chosen her over death.

Would she be all right with an elishina? He had never explained what it was or what it would mean for her since he had thought it so unlikely that one would form.

Yet the elishina would affect Essie more than it did him. Hopefully she would not despise him when she found out.

That would explain Weylind's increasingly deep scowl. He, of course, was not happy about the elishina. Not if it meant that Farrendel would give up hundreds of years of his life for Essie.

Farrendel turned back to Rheva. "What does our elishina"—that was strange to say—"have to do with healing me?"

"Elspetha kept you alive, there on the battlefield. She used the deepest connection of the elishina to keep you breathing until I reached you and healed you enough to keep you alive." Rheva rested a hand on Essie's forehead, a hint of her green healing magic seeping into Essie. "But she is human. Keeping you alive and activating the deep connection of the elishina was a great strain on her body. Right now, her body is sustaining yours, and yours is sustaining hers."

"Should I let go of her hand?" Farrendel held up their clasped hands again. If he remembered the legends right, the deep connection of an elishina was strongest when the couple was touching. If he let her go, that would disconnect the deep elishina so that he was no longer putting strain on Essie.

"No, not yet." Rheva wrapped her hand over his and Essie's clasped fingers. "The elishina needs time to settle into her body, and I believe it would be best if we let it run its course. Once she is rested, she will wake perfectly fine, and then you will be able to pull away safely. Until then, we will tend your wounds as much as we can without further straining Essie, then we will let both of you rest until we can heal you the rest of the way when she wakes."

Farrendel nodded and tried to relax. "Whatever is best for Essie."

Weylind made a noise in the back of his throat. As if he thought Rheva should heal Farrendel all the way, no matter what strain it might put on Essie.

Rheva shot a glare at him over her shoulder. "You are not helping. Please leave us to our work and see to preparing the train for our departure."

With one last, pained glance at Farrendel, Weylind spun on his heels and marched from the room.

After Weylind left, Rheva and Arorien's healer set to work cleaning Farrendel's wounds and picking out the pieces of his shirt that had been lodged inside him.

He gritted his teeth through the process, focusing on holding back his magic and trying not to let the pain affect Essie.

Finally, they re-bandaged the wounds, and the healer settled a slow healing magic on the wounds.

Rheva rested her hand on Farrendel's forehead.

Before she could use her magic to send him back to sleep, he shook his head. "Not yet. I need to speak with Weylind."

Rheva hesitated for a moment before she nodded. She headed for the door, shutting it quietly after her.

Farrendel glanced at Essie lying next to him. She still slept, but, now that his wounds were tended and the healing magic numbed his pain, the lines had smoothed from her face.

The door opened again, and Weylind stepped inside. Grooves still dug deeply into his face. His dark eyes searched Farrendel's face. "Shashon?"

"I am fine, Weylind." Or he would be, once the healers could finish their work.

Farrendel glanced at Essie again, then held up their

clasped hands. "Do not grieve, shashon. This is what I want."

Weylind sighed as he braced his hands against the table. "Machasheni Leyleira was right, it seems. You and Essie are like Daesyn and Inara, with both their joys and their sorrows."

"Perhaps." But Farrendel was not grieving the loss of a few hundred years of his life. For Essie, it was beyond worth it. "I know this is not what you wanted for me. But, please, all I ask is that you try to accept Essie. She is not an Escarlish spy or assassin or anything you thought she might be. She is not going to make my life miserable. After all, an elishina can only form from both sides."

For a long moment, Weylind did not move. Then, he nodded and lifted his gaze to meet Farrendel's. "Very well, shashon. I will do better where Elspetha is concerned. She has proven that she has a heart as fierce as any elven warrior."

A fierce heart. Shynafir. It suited Essie. She loved fiercely, so fiercely that she had seen his scars, his nightmares, his darkness, and still loved him.

Weylind opened his mouth as if he planned to say something more, then he shook his head again. He pushed away from the table. "I will fetch Rheva. Let her use her magic to help you rest. It will be a long train ride to Estyra, and we will have much to attend to when we return."

Farrendel nodded, already letting himself drift as Weylind strode out and Rheva stepped back in. Yes, they would have a lot to deal with when they returned. But until then, he would rest. Essie was alive. He was alive. Right now, that was more than he could have dared hoped for.

CHAPTER TWENTY

F arrendel relaxed in the peaceful warmth between sleep and wakefulness. The bed below him was soft and was no longer moving as the train glided its way through the Tarenhieli forest.

But he was not alone. As he woke, he became aware of Essie lying in the bed next to him. He was not entirely sure how he could be so certain it was her. Perhaps it was the whiff of the floral scent of the conditioner she had picked out at Illyna's. Maybe it was the tickle of her hair against his cheek.

Or maybe it was the elishina settled deep in his chest that made him so attuned to her.

Beside him, Essie drew in a deep breath and shifted. Waking up. She did not seem to be in any pain, so Rheva must have been right that Essie would wake just fine.

Essie shifted again, his only warning, before her fingers trailed through a strand of his hair.

It took all of his self-control to remain still, even though his muscles nearly stiffened and his breath wanted to catch in his throat. In his first panic, he was torn between the instinct to pull away and the strengthening urge to relax at her touch.

For the past few years, he had never thought he would ever want to allow anyone close enough to enjoy the intimacies of marriage. It seemed too dangerous to sleep with someone in the same room, much less share a bed. And everything else just seemed...awkward. Kissing sounded more than a little disgusting if one thought about it too much.

But this was Essie. And, somehow, that made everything different than what he had expected. No, he was not yet ready for everything that came with marriage. But he was ready to start working that way. Including getting up the nerve to finally kiss her.

Essie's fingers moved from his hair to tracing along his pointed ear. Her touch was so light and ticklish that he could not stay still, pretending to be asleep, any longer. "Why are you touching my ear?"

His skin felt cold as she snatched her hand back. "I... um...your ear is pointed. I've been curious ever since I married you and...sorry."

When he turned toward her and peeled his eyes open, he caught the adorably pink flush that stole across her face. He did not get to see her flustered often—he was usually the bewildered one—so he would enjoy this moment while it lasted.

He might even try to get her a bit more flustered while he was at it. Right now, he was filled with a reckless, unfettered kind of bravery that urged him to say whatever uncensored thing came out of his mouth first. With Essie, he had the freedom to do that without worrying that he would embarrass himself too badly. "Do all humans find pointed ears attractive?"

Her mouth curled into that bright smile he loved so much, though this one had an edge of flirtation to it that made his head spin a bit. "I don't know. Maybe. I do, apparently."

He took in her smiling face for another moment before he sighed and looked away. As much as he wanted to rest here with Essie, they had business to attend to. Weylind would be arranging a council meeting to discuss the ambushes and the weapons used during that second battle on the trail.

Weapons that he could now see were very human—probably Escarlish—weapons.

That would explain the mysterious raids. The trolls had been sneaking across the border, not to raid villages but to claim the weapons from a smuggler.

A smuggler who had to be an elf.

That meant both an elven traitor and a human traitor were involved, assuming that Essie's brother Averett wasn't purposely sending weapons to the trolls through the elven traitor.

No, surely not. King Averett loved his sister. He would not put her in peril by giving weapons to the trolls.

But Weylind would not see it that way. He would only see Escarlish weapons in the hands of Tarenhiel's enemies.

Farrendel pushed onto his elbows. Pain stabbed into his stomach, far sharper than he had expected, and he collapsed back onto his pillow with a gasp.

Right. He was still wounded. The elven healing magic had dulled the pain, but the slow healing had not done as much as he had expected during the hours he slept.

Essie bolted upright, her eyes searching his face. "Do you need me to get you anything? A drink? Painkiller? I don't know where anyone is, but I'm sure someone is around who can fetch the physician. Or healer I guess you call them."

She shoved the blanket aside, letting go of his hand for the first time.

The loss of the deep connection of the elishina left him breathless. As she made to stand up, he reached out and gripped her arm in a surge of panic. For some undefinable reason, he was not yet ready to have her leave. "No, please stay."

She halted, her forehead still wrinkled with worry. "Are you sure?"

"Yes. I am fine." He was fine enough, anyway. And he would be fine just as soon as he was healed the rest of the way. Essie seemed to be recovered from any ill-effects of the elishina. "I am used to being healed more than this when I wake up. It is fine."

Perhaps it would not hurt if he rested a few minutes longer before he was healed and they went in search of Weylind. This moment with Essie was too precious to cut short.

Essie lay back down next to him, propped up on one elbow facing him. "All right. But the moment you look like the pain is getting to you, I'm going to find the healer."

Then he would just make sure she did not see any of the lingering pain.

Besides, he did not want to think about pain right now. Not while Essie was lying next to him, and he was still gripped by that they-both-survived-and-he-did-not-want-to-waste-time recklessness. He reached for her hand again, lacing their fingers together. "You saved my life."

"I did? I kind of thought you saved mine. That last blast of your magic was incredible. I thought we were all going to die there. But I guess I did save you when I shot the trolls by the repeater gun. None of the elves could shoot back without exposing themselves to fire." Essie ran her thumb over the back of Farrendel's hand, sending shivers up his arm and down his spine. He was not sure she was even aware of what she was doing to him.

He forced himself to focus on her and not on the way his heart was beating harder in his throat.

She had faced battle for the first time. She had killed. In the moment, she had been focused and determined, but he knew firsthand how such things could hit later after the moment of danger was past.

He reached up and touched her cheek, her skin so soft beneath his fingers. "How are you doing? It was your first battle."

She shifted a little closer, but her gaze swung away from his and dropped to their clasped hands instead. "Honestly, I haven't thought about it much. I woke up only a few minutes before you did, and on the battlefield when you were hit, I just did what I had to do."

"If it hits you later or you have nightmares, I will be here." After all, she had been there often enough for him. The least he could do was return the favor, though he hoped for her sake that her nightmares were far more mild than his.

"I know." Her voice softened as her eyes flicked back up to meet his. Sometime in the last few moments, she had leaned closer, as had he, until their faces were inches apart.

This was it. It was not the romantic moment at Lethorel that he had envisioned, but it was time to quit stalling.

But what if she did not want him to kiss her? What if she was not ready for that yet? What if—

She trailed her fingers through his hair again. "When I thought we were all going to die, I regretted that I'd never kissed you. I know you elves aren't ones to kiss before you truly love someone and all that, but I—"

That was all the permission he needed. No more over-thinking this.

He kissed her.

And it turned out, he liked kissing. A lot. At least when he was kissing Essie.

He wrapped an arm around her waist and pulled her closer, his other hand cradling her face. Just out of curiosity, he trailed his finger over her ear. But it did not feel any different from his, so he was not sure what had her so fascinated with his pointed ears.

Not that it mattered much while he was kissing her.

She eased away, her breathing coming fast.

His was too, and a stab of pain broke through the haze of kissing. He pressed a hand to the bandages around his waist. These injuries sure were becoming a nuisance.

"Sorry. You're in pain." Essie pulled even farther away, a frown replacing her smile. "Maybe we should hold off on kissing until you're finished healing."

Now that sounded like a horrible idea. If anything, he thought kissing more might make him forget all about his gunshot wounds.

"Depends on how long the healer takes to finish healing me." That even sounded a bit flirtatious. He found himself smiling.

Essie laughed, the smile returning. "I like kissing you too."

Well, that was a relief. Apparently, he had not done it wrong.

For a moment, they lapsed into a quiet, comfortable silence.

This was what love was like. It could be charged and heated like a moment ago. Or it could be soft and comfortable. It was the freedom to be himself without worrying about his awkwardness, and the joy of giving Essie that same freedom in return.

Even though the deep connection of the elishina had ended, he could still sense her deep inside his chest. A warm and joyful presence that banished the weight inside him.

The elishina. He had started to explain earlier, but then he had gotten a little...distracted.

His smile faded as he searched her face. He should not put this off. She needed to know just what had happened at the end of the battle. "When I said you saved my life, I did not only mean when you shot those trolls. I was dying, and you did not let go. We elves call that an *elishina*. Heart-bonded."

"*Elishina*? What do you mean? How did I save you then? I'm not even sure what happened." Essie flopped back onto her pillow, though she lay closer than before.

How did he even go about explaining it? Perhaps he should start at the beginning. "Do you remember in our wedding ceremony when we pledged that our hearts would be as one?"

Essie nodded. "There was this zing of magic, at least I think that's what it was."

"When we elves marry, we become very literally and

magically bonded. Sometimes, the bond is so deep that if one is injured, the other's heart can literally keep beating for both of them." He stared at the ceiling rather than look at her, though he squeezed her hand to make sure she knew he was not ignoring her. "I was not sure it would happen with us. The only human and elf pair to experience it was Daesyn and Inara, and even then, it was the elf's heart beating for the human's."

Though Machasheni had seemed sure they would form an elishina, even from the beginning. He was not sure what Machasheni had seen in them that would convince her, but she had that way about her. Perhaps it came from being over eight hundred years old.

Essie propped herself on her elbow again. "So when I gripped your hand and it felt like I was struggling to breathe, it was because I was breathing for you?"

Ugh. He was not doing a good job of explaining it. "Sort of. More like as long as you were breathing, I would stay breathing, and as long as your heart was beating, mine would be too."

Her eyes brightened with the light of understanding, and she gave a small nod.

Giving in to temptation, he pushed a strand of hair from her face, letting the silken red strands slide through his fingers. He had come so close to losing her, both in the battle and due to her valiant efforts to keep him alive. "You could have died if the strain of keeping me alive had been too much. Before I met you, I never would have expected a human's heart could sustain an elf's that way."

Rather than sober her, Essie smiled, shaking her head. "We humans may be reckless and make a lot of mistakes, but when we love, we love fiercely. Our lives are too short to afford to do anything less."

"We elves could probably learn something from you about making each day count." Even an elf's life could be short. His had nearly been cut short several times already. He cradled her face, searching her eyes. "I hoped on the day I married you that we would form a heart bond." Well, that was stretching it a little bit. Machasheni had hoped, and she had helped him have a smidgen of hope. So it was true enough. "But I did not expect, if it would happen, that it would occur this soon. We had not even kissed before the battle."

"Maybe we hadn't kissed, but both of us have been choosing to love each other from the day we married." Essie held his gaze, tilting her head to lean into his hand. "Love is a choice, and it's one we have been making all along. That probably counts a whole lot more for a heart bond than kissing does, even if I'm discovering I really like kissing you."

He rather liked kissing her too. And he might have done it again, except that he still had yet to explain the consequence of the elishina that would most affect her. "Will it bother you if your life is longer than what is expected for a human?"

He held his breath, waiting for her answer.

Instead of pain or surprise, her forehead scrunched. She sighed and flopped back onto the pillow. "What do you mean? This has something to do with Daesyn and Inara again, doesn't it? I think it's high time I heard that whole story."

Of course she was struggling to understand. She did not know the elven legends the way he did.

He lay back and clasped her hand again. "Inara was a princess of the elves, and Daesyn was a human woodsman. They met and fell in love. Daesyn helped the elven king, Inara's father, push the trolls back into the northern realms, and he was wounded in the last, great battle. Inara's heart bond with him kept him alive until the healers could save him. Their heart bond was so strong that Daesyn lived to nearly five hundred years old. Inara died shortly after he did, young for an elf. The stories say she gave her years to him, and that's how he lived for so long."

For a moment, Essie remained silent, staring at the ceiling. He could not read the emotions and thoughts that flickered across her face and in her eyes.

When she finally spoke, her voice was quiet and sober. "This is why your family was so concerned about you falling in love with me. They feared that either we wouldn't form a heart bond and your heart would be broken when I died in only a short time compared to an elf's years or we would form this special bond and you would end up dying young. They don't want to lose you."

And there was his Essie. The first concern she voiced was not about outliving her own family, but about him dying young compared to his.

"No, they do not. But, Essie." Farrendel pushed himself onto an elbow, ignoring the twinge of pain in his middle. He needed to look into her eyes as he said this. "I would gladly give up a few hundred years if it meant that the years I did have were spent with you."

Hopefully that sounded more romantic to Essie than it did in his own ears.

She smiled and leaned closer, their faces so close once

again that their breaths mingled. "And I would happily live to be five hundred if I'm with you."

And as that seemed as good an invitation to kiss her again as any, he closed the distance and did just that. He buried his fingers in her hair, silken and slightly curling in a way elven hair did not.

Kissing her the second time was even better than the first. If practice made kissing better, then he was more than happy to practice kissing as much as Essie wanted.

He drew back enough to murmur, "I think I am in love with you."

She grinned right back at him, her cheeks pink and her eyes bright. "I should hope so. I know I'm in love with you."

They had come a long way from their arranged marriage, where all he had dared hope was that their marriage would not be miserable.

He had not known how to hope for *this*. Loving and being loved in return.

He was not yet sure how to dream for a future after so long of expecting none. He did not know how to truly *live* after simply existing day after day.

But with Essie, he might have a hope of figuring it out.

FREE BOOK!

Thanks so much for reading *Elf Prince*! I hope this glimpse into Farrendel's thoughts during the events of *Fierce Heart* brought a smile. If you loved the book, please consider leaving a review. Reviews help your fellow readers find books that they will love.

A downloadable map and a downloadable list of characters and elvish are available on the Extras page of my website.

If you ever find typos in my books, feel free to message me on social media or send me an email through the Contact Me page of my website.

If you want to learn about all my upcoming releases, get great book recommendations, and see a behind-the-scenes glimpse into the writing process, follow my blog at www.taragrayce.com.

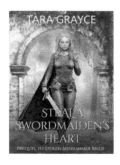

Did you know that if you sign up for my newsletter, you'll receive lots of free goodies? You will receive the free novella *Steal a Swordmaiden's Heart*, which is set in the same world as *Stolen Midsummer Bride* and *Bluebeard and the Outlaw*! This novella is a prequel to *Stolen Midsummer Bride*, and tells the story of how King Theseus of the Court of

Knowledge won the hand of Hippolyta, Queen of the Swordmaidens.

You will also receive the free novellas *The Wild Fae Primrose* (prequel to *Forest of Scarlet*) and *Torn Curtains*, a fantasy Regency Beauty and the Beast retelling.

Sign up for my newsletter now

'IN THE MOOD FOR FAE
FANTASY?

FOREST OF SCARLET

The fae snatch humans as playthings to torment. The Primrose steals them back.

Vowing that no other family would endure the same fear and pain she felt when her older sister was snatched by the fae, Brigid puts on an empty-headed façade while she rescues humans in the shadowy guise of the Primrose, hero to humans, bane to the fae. Her only regret is that she can't tell the truth to Munch, the young man in the human realm who she's trying very hard not to fall in love with.

Munch has a horrible nickname, an even more terrible full name, and the shadow of his heroic sister and five older brothers to overcome. It's rough being the little brother of the notorious Robin Hood and her merry band. The highlights of his life are the brief visits by Brigid, the messenger girl for the dashing fae hero the Primrose.

When an entire village of humans is snatched by the fae in a single night, Munch jumps at the chance to go to the Fae Realm, pass a message to Brigid and through her to the Primrose, and finally get his chance to be a hero just like all his older siblings.

But the Fae Realm is a dangerous place, especially for a human unbound to a fae or court like Munch. One wrong decision could spell disaster for Munch, Brigid, and the Primrose.

Will this stolen bride's sister and Robin Hood's brother reveal the truth of their hearts before the Fae Realm snatches hope away from them forever?

Loosely inspired by *The Scarlet Pimpernel*, *Forest of Scarlet* is book one in a new fantasy romance / fantasy romantic comedy series of standalones featuring magic libraries, a whimsical and deadly fae realm, and crazy fae hijinks by bestselling author Tara Grayce!

Find the Book on Amazon Today!

ALSO BY TARA GRAYCE

ELVEN ALLIANCE

Fierce Heart

War Bound

Death Wind

Troll Queen

Pretense

Shield Band

Elf Prince

Peril: Elven Alliance Collected Stories Volume One

Inventor: Elven Alliance Collected Stories Volume Two

COURT OF MIDSUMMER MAYHEM

Stolen Midsummer Bride (Prequel)

Forest of Scarlet

Night of Secrets

A VILLAIN'S EVER AFTER

Bluebeard and the Outlaw

PRINCESS BY NIGHT

Lost in Averell

ACKNOWLEDGMENTS

Thank you to everyone who made this book possible! To my writer friends, especially Molly, Morgan, Addy, Savannah, Sierra, and the entire Spinster Aunt gang for being so encouraging and helpful. To my dad for being willing to drop anything to read early copies of my books. To my mom for always encouraging me. To my sisters-in-law Alyssa and Abby for adoring Essie and Farrendel. To my friends Paula, Bri, and Jill for always listening when I ramble about stories. To my proofreaders Tom, Mindy, and Deborah, thanks so much for helping to eradicate the typos as much as humanly possible!

But thanks especially to my Heavenly Father who brought me through some difficult times this past year.

Milton Keynes UK
Ingram Content Group UK Ltd.
UKHW022005110823
426759UK00019B/235/J